MW01532622

Caleb's Sojourn

guy carey jr.

PublishAmerica
Baltimore

© 2008 by guy carey jr.
All rights reserved. No part of this book may be reproduced, stored in a retrieval system or transmitted in any form or by any means without the prior written permission of the publishers, except by a reviewer who may quote brief passages in a review to be printed in a newspaper, magazine or journal.

First printing

All characters in this book are fictitious, and any resemblance to real persons, living or dead, is coincidental.

PublishAmerica has allowed this work to remain exactly as the author intended, verbatim, without editorial input.

ISBN: 1-60610-977-4
PUBLISHED BY PUBLISHAMERICA, LLLP
www.publishamerica.com
Baltimore

Printed in the United States of America

This book is dedicated to all those readers who keep asking what happens in the rest of Caleb's life. To my first readers Colleen Paul and Arline Vanderstelt and my wife Cathie and all the rest of my family for their encouragement and help. A very special thanks goes to my daughter-in-law Lynn Carey who does my editing.

PROLOGUE

This book Caleb's Sojourn completes the trilogy started with The Town Barn Isn't There Anymore and Caleb, Caleb, Caleb. The first book chronicles Caleb Carney's life as a young boy growing up in the 1930 and 40s. The second book records his struggles in accepting the responsibilities of entering adulthood. The third book Caleb's Sojourn is Caleb's story as a student, husband, father and breadwinner, clearly showing the mark of his life from the first two books.

Chapter 1

It seemed as if we had just left Lynbrook and here we were in Lotus driving into the college campus.

"Well, Caleb! I guess this is it, the start of your journey into the world of higher education," Eunice said. "I believe that you are better prepared now than you were last year. I hear that sometimes it's good to spend a year out in the world between high school and college."

Though I was thankful that my sister and her family lived close to the college and that I had a chance to work for a while in her husband's contracting business, my year off hadn't lessened the fear I felt about leaving the life I had in Sterling. Still, Eunice and I had been apart too long for me to really feel like confiding all my fears to her.

"I'm going to miss you and Harry and especially little Hank," I told her. "He's become quite a boy since I left."

"You don't need to miss us. Just as soon as you have some time here and get organized with your room and classes, you can come spend a weekend with us," Eunice replied, giving me a little kiss as I got out and grabbed my gear.

Even though my new home away from home wasn't an enormous building, the impact of entering it the first time as my home for the next four years seemed enormous. The room I was to share was on the third floor. Not trusting my knowledge of how to use an elevator, I climbed the stairs. As I slowly climbed, each step seemed more a dragging away than an ascending to some great new adventure in life. Away from what I knew, from friends and family. Good-bye my town of Sterling, good-bye my mountain, good-bye to a life where I had finally found a comfortable niche.

The few days I had spent with Eunice and Harry hadn't done much to shake the shackles of the preceding year, when I had rushed back just before getting here last fall because of my father's accident. The fear after seeing how badly he was hurt, the obligatory decision to take his place. The luck of having Norman and Bruce as my left and right arm while managing Dad's small part in the lumber business. The rejoining of the boys and girls of my young life, a life that I thought was gone forever. The thrill, the ignominy and confusion of being linked again with the girls I had grown up with and the realization that life wasn't a kid's game anymore.

As I climbed the last stairway away from all of that, the stairs seemed somehow steeper and longer and each step a little harder, as if my whole being was fighting the realization that my new world at the top of the stairs was taking that away from me.

Just as I reached the top of that stairway, I heard someone say, "Hey, kid, let me help you with that. Didn't you ever hear of elevators? You look like you're about to have a heart attack carrying all that weight. What room are you headed for?"

"Three ten." I answered. "But I'm all right, just a little confused, that's all."

"I'll be damned, that's my room too. My name's Thomas Jones, but you can call me Tom or Jones if you like. That's what our other roommate calls me. Here's our room. Hey, Warren! Here's our new roommate. I didn't catch your name yet, did I?" he asked thoughtfully.

"I'm sorry," I answered. "Name's Caleb Carney. Here to major in journalism. I was supposed to start last year but I had to go home and take my father's place until he could return to work after an accident."

"Well! Caleb Carney," Tom said, introducing me. "This here is Warren Weld and we are both here studying to become engineers, him in civil engineering and me in electrical. You look kind of young to be here on the GI bill. What did you do? Lie about your age to get in the service?"

"No, I wasn't in the service," I answered, thinking, *I don't think I should tell them about Josh, at least not now.* "My tuition is being paid by money left in the will of one of my grammar school teachers who thought I had promise."

"You know what, Tom?" Warren chimed in, laughing. "Maybe we could get him to write some of the papers we hate so much."

"I wouldn't count on that," I answered. "It took my friend Jake hours to help me convert my writings to real English."

"Come on, Warren," Tom shouted. "Let's get out of here and let our young friend get settled. Sorry about the crowded conditions, Caleb, but there are so many GI Joes trying to get smart enough to never have to go to war again, the colleges are all swamped. What they have done here is convert every two-student room that was big enough into a three-student room."

I had just finished stuffing my gear when Jake came busting into the room, shouting, "Found you, Caleb! I asked at the administration office for your room number. If you're all settled here let me take you for a tour of the campus."

Jake rushed me around the campus, pointing out the buildings where my classes would be held. He was still all fired up about college. He apologized for rushing me but said he was due at a meeting where they were discussing world affairs, and encouraged me to join him.

"Not tonight," I said. "I have some writing to do and I'm not ready to mix right yet."

"Okay, but you had better get up to speed in a hurry so we can spend time together. I'm involved in a number of these kind of meetings," he said as he rushed off.

It seemed Jake hadn't changed much since we went to school in Sterling. He always loved classes where we were allowed to debate. Funny how we became such good friends after Hanna got us working together.

College was hard for me, the classes were so large and the lectures required studious note taking, and that had never been my forte. Still, I manage to struggle through and at least get decent, although not remarkable, grades. I hadn't found much time to spend with Jake. It seemed every time

I had time he was busy at his meetings. I tried going with him a couple of times but all of the politicking was too much for me.

Rooming with Tom and Warren turned out to be okay. They were both too used to crowded barracks life to be bothered by our close quarters. Besides, none of us spent much time there except for sleeping.

For me, it was classes and the library. I'm not sure how they spent their time. After a couple of months I called Eunice and she came and got me so I could spend a weekend at their house. I called Shaq but he wasn't home. I was disappointed because I was hoping to see Etta again. I hadn't gone to parties around the college much. The couple of times I had, the drinking and carrying on was too scary for me, although some of the girls were tempting.

When I got back to the college, Tom said, "It looks like we're either going to have more room in here or a new roommate. Warren got some kind of a contagious disease from one of the cute little girls he has been running around with and the damn fool went to the college sickbay for help and they kicked him out. Boy, was he ripping! He kept muttering he had screwed everything available all around the world only to get taken down back home by some cute college girl. He doesn't dare to go home to his family so he is going some place the college recommended for a cure."

"That's too bad. I hope he gets better," I answered, thinking, *I guess I should erase thoughts of those tempting girls from my mind; I sure don't want that to happen to me.*

The next few months were full of the same thing over and over: study, write papers, go to class, go to the library, and my room. Just before summer vacation one of my professors called me in for a conference. I was kind of scared to go, but it was mandatory.

After waiting nervously outside of his office for almost half an hour, his secretary finally said, "Professor White will see you now."

As I walked in he said, "Mr. Carney, we need to talk about your work. You have a vivid way of describing things but it worries me that most of your writing is about childhood things. You need to expand beyond that if you want to be taken seriously as a correspondent. I would suggest that you use your summer working on that. I am not criticizing you, just suggesting where you need improvement. You may have talent as a novelist but that is not what you are studying. And trying to become a successful novelist in today's world is a risky career choice."

I thanked the professor for his suggestions and hurried out of there, relieved that it wasn't worse than that. He had already noted the same thing on some of my papers. I guess he thought I wasn't improving in that vein. I had tried, but he claimed I didn't show much authority in the papers I did about things other than my own experiences.

The rest of my college year was uneventful and suddenly I was faced with the decision of how and where I was going to spend my summer.

Harry had already asked me to work with his steel crew. He had two buildings under construction and needed more men, and since I had a little experience on his jobs he thought I would be a benefit.

I really wanted to go back to Sterling but Homer had already written me saying he hoped I wasn't planning on going back to sticking lumber because he hated to see Norman and Bruce broken up as a team. He had written that Dad brags about how smart I was in leaving him with such capable workers. I already had figured out I might cause a problem if I went home to Sterling so I told Harry I'd work the summer with him if I could go home for a few days after classes.

I was able to get a train for Oscin out of Lotus the same day classes ended, so I took a taxi to the station. For the first time I sat in a train listening to the click clack of the tracks with joy instead of dread. In Oscin, Homer was at the station waiting in the '41 Chevy. I had completely forgotten that he had his license now and I felt a pang of jealousy seeing him drive my car. I hadn't been home since last fall because Harry had needed me during the Christmas break. Homer seemed so much more grown up.

He finally spotted me standing there, lost in thought. "Hey, Caleb, have you been studying so hard you're blind?" he hollered. "I thought you were looking right through me."

"No, Homer, it's just I am so thrilled to be back that I was just taking it all in," I answered with a laugh.

"Well," Homer replied, "you better not waste your time daydreaming! Everyone is waiting for you. We even got a call from Joan's parents. She heard you were coming and will be home tomorrow and wants to see you right away."

Joan and I had written a few times during the year. Her last letter seemed rather vague for her. I hope her "right away" wasn't too ominous.

11

I gave Homer a slap on the back, saying, "How are things? Are you still the king of the kissing club?"

As we climbed into the car, Homer said, "Not so much any more. In high school I found that could be trouble. One time I was called into the principal's office because two girls got in a fight over me. When I tried to talk to one of them afterward I got my face slapped, so I decided it was best to give it up."

At home, Mother had made my favorite dinner. At the dinner table everyone had questions about college. I put a little more enthusiasm in my answers than I felt. It only seemed fair, as they were so excited for me. They filled me in about the family. Francis was helping out with the chores now that his allergies were under control. That had allowed Jason to work sometimes at Muldon's barn when they were shorthanded.

Aaron, Hester's intended, had finished his degree and though they hadn't set a date they were making plans for a wedding as soon as Aaron knew where he was going to be assigned by his company. Dad still had a noticeable limp but he seemed to accept that as good, considering they had talked about removing his leg right after the accident. Homer had one more year in high school and was considering going on with his education in the field of welding, as he had been doing some of this for the Muldons.

After supper Nellie walked with me around the farm.

As we were coming back in she said, "You're not as happy as you tried to act in there, huh, Caleb?"

I laughed and answered, "I should have known that you would see right through me, Nellie. But it isn't that bad. It's just that coming home reminded me how different and perplexing the outside world can be."

"It's funny how different you boys are," Nellie said. "Both Jason and Homer are waiting their chance to go out in the world where you seem to only need little Sterling to complete your world. I know you won't be here only a few days, but Mother has a money problem that she could use some advice on, so make sure you spend some time with her."

I spent the rest of the day with the family, and got up early the next day to take Dad to work so I could have the car. It was great to see Norman and Bruce but we didn't have much time to talk because they had to go to work. I stopped to have a coffee with Virginia, leaving after about half an hour, thinking what a great thing it was the she and Norman had met.

Back home I went in to see Mother and asked her, "What kind of money problem are you having?"

She laughed and said, "It's getting to be impossible to have a secret with Nellie around. We don't have a problem with lack of money, its just the opposite, with all that was collected and the money Hester and Richard are still sending home. Now there is considerable money, even after all the bills are paid. Mr. Banner suggested that we bank some in case Dad needs it later, and that I should take at least half of it and put it toward our mortgage. Hester had suggested that we use some of it to give Emma a good wedding but Aaron feels being married at the farm should become a Carney tradition, and that is how he and Emma want to get married."

"You know, Mother," I answered, relieved that it was an abundance and not a lack of money, "I think we can rely on Mr. Banner's advice. He has managed the money well for us and has more expertise about money than any of us. I would tell Hester and Richard, but there isn't anyone else I think who has to be informed. I know most of this has been kept from Dad but when the time comes he has to know, he'll be all right with it."

After spending a couple of hours with Mother, I called Joan's house.

Much to my surprise she answered the phone. "Caleb, I'm so glad you called! I was wondering if it would be possible for you to take me over to see Virginia? I know neither one of us is going to be home long and I need to see her."

"The only time I would have to do that would be today. Could you go now?" I asked, feeling ominous about her request.

"That's great. I can be ready in five minutes. I'll see you then," she answered, and then hung up.

Joan came running out as soon as I drove into her yard. I marveled at how she looked. This wasn't my little Joan anymore. She had blossomed into a very attractive woman in the two years she had been in college.

She gave me a little kiss and sat quietly, and seemed to study me for some time before finally saying, "Caleb, do you think there will ever be an 'us'?"

"Hell," I exploded. "What kind of a question is that, the first time we meet after being apart for so long?"

"Don't be mad. It's just that I've been thinking about us and your no-commitment spiel and I'm not sure that it would be smart for me to be

13

spending my best years just sitting around waiting for something if it can never be. After all, you can't expect a girl to be happy just being part of a harem, can you?" she asked, giving me a little hug.

I was at a loss as to what to say. What popped into my head was what Homer and Emma had said about Joan and her mother.

So I said, "I'm not sure how to answer you, Joan. I know we can't stay the little kids we were as much as I would like to, but I'm still not ready to make a commitment, if that's your question."

"I guess that's what I'm asking. I had some hope that college would change that about you. Then I wondered if you would still be you, if it did. Oh, hell! Caleb, let's drop all this baloney and see if we can find ice cream on our way," she said with a laugh.

"We're almost there, and there isn't any place to buy ice cream around here. I kind of wish there was. Maybe we can find some on the way back," I said as we turned into the road to the lot.

Joan hurried up to Norman and Virginia's shanty and I went down to the mill to see Dad and the boys. We had a great time laughing about all the things we had been through the year before, especially the pig roast and the shivaree at Norman's wedding party.

I felt comfortable here and too soon it was time to go home. I knew I had other obligatory visits to make, and I had promised Harry that I would be back in a few days.

Joan and I headed back to Sterling, both forgetting about looking for ice cream.

"I have to leave tomorrow by noon," Joan said. "Can we get together later today?"

"I'll try," I answered, "but it will be late. I promised the Harts I would have supper with them. They want me to catch up on Karl and his new family."

Joan was quiet most of the rest of the way home.

When we arrived at her house, she gave me a little kiss and said, "Is it Karl or Betty that you're interested in catching up with?"

Without waiting for an answer she angrily rushed into the house.

I drove off wondering if I even wanted to return. Joan had been acting strange all day and the last thing I needed was to get caught up in that harem bunk again.

When I arrived at the Harts, Betty's intended, George Tilton, was already there and we had a chance to talk before Betty came home. He seemed like a nice guy and I was happy for Betty.

We spent a long evening talking about Karl and our escapades growing up in Sterling. They told George about how I had helped Karl after he had been wounded and that I had probably saved Betty's life. Betty kind of rolled her eyes and smiled. Seeing her and remembering those stories not only brought back memories, it kindled some of the wild desires she was so good at creating.

It was so late when I left the Harts I didn't bother to go to Joan's house. I called in the morning but her mother said she was too busy to come to the phone.

I spent the next couple of days visiting most of my old haunts and friends. Harry called to remind me that I was needed on his job. I told him I had planned to leave the next day and gave him the time the train would be in Lotus so Eunice could pick me up.

I had to drive to the job to pick up Dad so he could leave the truck for Norman. Dad had told me that Virginia had asked for me to come a little early, as she wanted to talk to me.

When I got to the job site, I went up to see Virginia.

"I'm glad you could make it," she said. "It's been a long time since we had time to talk. I have given a lot of thought to talking to you about Joan's visit but I've decided it is the right thing to do. Her concern is sort of about the rape but in a way, it is more about recovering from it. She's been thinking about you and how you two have been close for so long. Seems that Joan has finally found someone else she is attracted to besides you and she's worried about how she will be able handle any sexual advances that might happen if she gets any closer to this guy and what she should do about you two."

"She has strong feelings for you, Caleb," Virginia continued. "But she doesn't feel as though you are capable of a long-term commitment. I didn't come right out and advise her what to do but we did talk a lot about how she might handle any sexual advances if she starts dating again. Though I didn't tell her this, if it had been anybody but you she was talking about, I would have advised her to cut and run. I'm telling you this not just for Joan's sake but also for your own because I think you need to hear it. I hope that I haven't overstepped my bounds and ruined our friendship. For whatever reason, many of your problems end up on my doorstep. I feel I should step in like a big sister would."

Though I was certainly taken aback by all that she had to say I knew that Virginia always had everyone's best interest at heart.

"I'm glad that you feel free to talk to me this way," I said. "I'm not sure that I grasp it all yet but it sure will be on my mind until I have. I knew Joan was very different the other day but I never would have guessed this. I'm glad Joan is thinking of dating someone else. It actually should make things between us easier, if nothing else. As children I was closer to Joan than any girl outside of my sisters but there was always the problem of her parents thinking I was trash. I know they have come down from that a bit lately, but like Homer says, she has been fed a steady diet about me being not good enough for years and if we ended up together I would pay for that. Still, the truth is that I don't think I have it in me to give unselfish love to anyone again after the pain I suffered when we lost Josh."

Just then Norman came busting in and said, "I hope you are charging him. Here he is home only a couple of days and he's bringing his harem and all that trouble back with him."

I put my arm around Norman's shoulder and said, "Come on, Norman, you wouldn't want Virginia charging one of your best friends, would you?"

"No, probably not," Norman answered. "Wish you had more time but your dad hurt his leg a little today and he asked me to hurry you up so he could leave."

I hurried back to the car. Dad was already sitting there waiting.

As I drove off Dad said, "Well, Caleb, what was the big predicament that Virginia had to see you about? She isn't planning to move, is she?"

"No, she just wanted to have a little time to talk before I left. By the way, Norman said you banged your leg today. What's with that?" I asked, feeling a little guilty about my answer.

"It's nothing. One of those big logs had a spot that the saw didn't get all the way through and when I went to snap it off it hit my leg. It was a little painful but no more than it would have been on my good leg, so don't worry or say anything to Mother," Dad said.

"I won't," I answered, making a mental note to have Emma and Aaron keep a watch on him to see if he was in any trouble.

I spent the evening with the family. I called Joan's parents and got her new address and I wrote to Jennie. Jennie and I had been corresponding regularly since she moved to New York.

> *Dear Jennie,*
>
> *I had a chance to spend a few days home, it was great to get home but Sterling isn't the same without you here. Betty has been taking classes at a community college and is doing well. She's thinking about going into nursing. I got a chance to meet her intended, George Tilton. He's nobody I knew from before but he seems like a good catch so I am happy for her. Joan asked me to take her to see Virginia and it seems she is dating someone at college. How my harem has dissipated! Shaq tells me Etta is planning a wedding soon too. With all my girlfriends deserting me, I guess I'll have to become a confirmed bachelor.*
>
> *I'm leaving for Oklahoma tomorrow. Harry needs me more than my family does now, so I am going to be working there for the summer. I plan to take a week off before I go back to college in the fall. I wish there was some way we could get together then. I know that this sounds like little Caleb running to you when he is in trouble with other girls but it isn't. I just wanted you to know how things are with me and to check up on you. Your last letter sounded a little wistful for the old days also and that worried me some, though I sure know the feeling. Write me soon at Harry and Eunice's address.*
>
> *With Love and Longing,*
> *Caleb*

The summer working with Harry was going fast. There wasn't much to do evenings so I went back to the club where I used to go with Shaq and Etta. The girls and boys there seemed a lot younger than I remembered and I felt out of place, so I went to the bar to order a soda.

To my surprise the girl behind the bar said, "Hey, Caleb, you look bewildered, but then most of Etta's castoffs end up looking that way. Did you get dumped too?"

It took me a minute but then I recalled her: June, the girl who I was sharing a Coke with the night Etta slapped it on the floor.

"No, June. Etta and I never became a couple, as desirable as that might have seemed sometimes. I was in the neighborhood and thought I'd stop and check out an old haunt before I went back to college. I'm surprised that everyone seems so much younger now. I guess that's what you are reading on my face."

June laughed and said, "Well I didn't get any younger, but I guess I wouldn't be here if I hadn't agreed to work the bar as a substitute when they needed me. I'm not allowed to leave the bar to dance but if you need company some other night, give me a call. As long as Etta's not here to bat us around, it might be fun."

I took my time finishing my soda. It seemed nice talking to June. Finally I got her number and promised I would call when I got back to Harry's house. I was glad I had stopped there because June and I dated several times during the rest of the summer and she was right—it was fun. We made arrangements to meet once in a while even after I went back to college. Good thing too, because all too soon I was back at school without even a full week off from my job.

Jennie and I had written often about seeing each other but there wasn't anyway either one of us could make the trip. Though she could get a few days off now and then, she said she was saving them up until she could arrange a trip when we both could be in Sterling.

I had new roommates in college but it was as if we didn't live on the same planet. It seemed all they were interested in was girls and parties. After seeing what those affairs did to Warren, I had given up on that life. College was the same as last year: class, library, and back to my room.

Come May though, I had something to be really excited about. Shaq had a friend who flew all over the place for the company he worked for. He owned his own plane and was going to be in the New York, close to where Jennie was working, for a week right after my last semester. Shaq had made arrangements for me to go with him. Harry said it would be all right but I wouldn't be able to go to Sterling until fall. I wrote to Jennie so she could arrange a place for me to stay and get that week off.

When I received her answer, I tore it open excitedly.

> *Dear Caleb,*
>
> *I am so excited! It has been such a long time. I have the use of one of the farm's vehicles occasionally and I asked if I could use it during my week off. They are very gracious to me here and worried about where I would be, but okayed the car. The airport where you are landing is half way to Tupper Lake where we stayed in the cottage the first time you brought me up here (remember?). I thought maybe it would be fun to stay at that lake. Remember how you told me about your Uncle Louis having worked in that area. I hope you don't think I'm too forward but if you can keep all the other girls out of your dreams, perhaps you'll be happier about our spending time together than you were then.*
>
> *More Than Just One Of Your Harem (I hope),*
> *Jennie*

The next week seemed endless. The thought that I was going to see Jennie again after over two years was so exhilarating, it kind of scared me. Who was Jennie now? Was she that teary-eyed passionate girl at the bus stop when she left? Or the caring warm compassionate young women who carried me through my anguish at losing Josh? Or the angry being that had so much trouble with me the summer before she left? I didn't care! All I cared about was we were going to be together for a week and there was joy in my heart.

I met Shaq's friend Earl at a small airport just outside of Lotus.

After Shaq had introduced us and Earl found out I had never flown, he said. "You're going to love this, Caleb. It's going to be great fun landing on the cow pasture of an airport where we are going."

"He's kidding, isn't he?" I asked.

"I don't really know, but if I was you I would buckle up good and tight anywhere I was flying with him," Shaq said with a laugh. "When he asked me if you were okay with his little plane I told him that you would do anything to have a chance to see your Jennie again. I think you even made Etta a little jealous when she heard me repeat that."

I had a little fear but I sure wasn't going to back out now, so I went with Earl to his plane. I didn't know enough about planes to know if it was little or not, but it had only two seats. I buckled in tight and we took off in a roar that drowned out any attempt to hold a conversation. After we leveled off it was better but we still had to yell. By the time we had arrived at our destination we both had tired of trying to be heard, so we didn't converse much.

As we circled below the clouds, Earl said, "See that flat area just beyond those hills? That's where we're going to land."

Now I wasn't just a little scared! I was scared as hell. I asked, "You're kidding, aren't you?"

"Don't worry, it will look bigger when you get down there. I've landed in much smaller places than this," he said with a laugh.

Earl brought the plane down so close to those hills that I couldn't look, so I held my seat with both hands and closed my eyes as we glided for a landing.

We landed so smooth and easy I couldn't believe it when Earl said, "It's okay, Caleb, you can open your eyes and let go of the seat. We are down safe and sound. Hey! Is that beautiful young lady beyond the fence your Jennie? Wow! No wonder you were willing to do anything to get here."

I had to agree with his "wow." It was hard to believe that Sterling's little barn girl was standing there.

"Earl, as scared as I was flying up here you have to promise me that anytime you come this way again you'll let me fly with you," I said.

"You know what?" he said with a laugh. "You're lucky I'm so much older than you or I might just fly up by myself to see if she would want to take flying lessons or something."

After making sure we had our dates and time straight for the fly back, I gave Earl a slap on the back and said, "You don't know how much this means to me, Earl. I haven't seen her in over two years and was afraid it was going be two more before I did."

After I had introduced Earl and Jennie, Earl walked away, but not before saying, "If I was you, I don't think I would even go back and take a chance she would wait for you two more years."

After he left Jennie and I just held each other without talking for the longest time.

Then one of the mechanics at a hanger hollered out, "Hey, you two go find a motel or something. I can't get my partner to do anything but stare at you and drool and we have work to do."

Jennie said, "I guess your reputation preceded you, Caleb. They already asked me if I was waiting for the college boy who was coming to the sticks to steal a pretty country girl."

"Shaq told me that Earl was known at all of the small air fields around this part of the world. I guess he must have said something to these guys when he logged in to land here," I answered as we got into the car.

The car was a prewar model but it showed the good care of someone who loved automobiles and ran like a charm, though it took some getting used to the mechanical brakes, as I hadn't driven anything like that since Dad's old truck. Jennie said it belonged to one of the Jolenes' sons who had gone into the service. He had agreed it would be okay if she used it after he watched her drive a few times.

As we rode along Jennie talked about her job and what being away from Sterling meant to her. "You know, as much as I missed some things in Sterling, up here it's like I am somebody, not just one of Muldon's barn girls," she said. "I am not expected to do any heavy lifting or go into any of the cow barns. My job now is mostly overseeing the work done in the milk room and to make sure everything is cleaned properly. The Jolenes are the nicest people to work for and if any of their workers get crude like the Muldon boys they straighten them out right away, or they're gone. I think if I had never known you I could settle down up here and be happy."

Though I could see her point it still bothered me that Jennie didn't have the attachment to Sterling that I did. Not wanting to get on that subject, I said, "Well, I'm happy for you, but I had hoped you had pined for me at least a little. So what's our big plan for the week besides Tupper Lake?"

Jennie whacked me one and said, "You can't believe that I would have agreed to this arrangement, Caleb Carney, if I hadn't missed you. As for plans, I haven't made any except how to escape you if I have to. I think it won't be any problem to find a good place to stay around the lake and just take it from there."

"Escape me? Why Jennie, why would you even have such thoughts? I believed from your letters over the last two years that that would have been the furthest thing from your mind. The real truth, though, is I have given a lot of thought about this trip and I want it to be as wonderful as we can make it. The way things are going in our lives, who knows when we can get together again and I want us both to have fond memories of this time together. As hard as it might seem or to believe, I'm willing to have separate bedrooms if that's what you want. Of course, I'll expect you to keep your kisses chaste all week so I can behave myself."

"Well, well, well," Jennie exclaimed. "What has college done to that wild Sterling boy who kept a big harem? You know what? I think I'll take you up on that just to see where it goes."

"That's okay, but no more of this harem business. Let's you and me have a new beginning and leave the past behind, at least the parts that are bothersome to us," I said, thinking maybe I was stating a little more than I intended.

"Look, Caleb," Jennie said. "There's a restaurant up ahead. You must be starved and I'm a little hungry myself. Let's stop. We don't want to start this adventure on an empty stomach."

It was only a little over an hour from the restaurant to the lake and Jennie actually fell asleep right after we left there. I woke her just before we got to the lake, after I started seeing signs for cabin rentals.

She was startled for a moment when she first woke up, then said, "I'm sorry, but the truth is I was too excited to sleep much last night. If we get a cabin not too close to the lake it will be cheaper and we can drive to the lake for anything we want to do there."

We stopped at the next group of cabins and asked for a two-bedroom. We were shown to a nice cabin that had two beds but one of them was in what was the kitchenette area. But it was clean and neat so we rented it for the week.

After unloading our gear we drove down to the lake.

Jennie spotted a sign advertising boat rides and said, "Let's do that. It will be more fun to see what's around here from a boat."

The boat ride was fun but the way Jennie cuddled up to me made me wonder how she expected me to keep this trip nonphysical. It was almost dark when we docked after the ride, so we ate at a place near the dock and then went back to our cabin.

22

At the cabin I asked, "Well, Jennie, who gets which bedroom?"

She just smiled and said, "Since I will probably be making the coffee and doing any cooking we do, I guess I should have the one in the kitchen."

The other room was very small and hardly had room for the bed and bureau. Right after cleaning up I lay down on the bed. I guess the airplane trip and all the excitement must have hit me because I fell asleep. I woke with a start and wondered what Jennie would think. Jennie was curled up on her bed, reading.

"I'm so-so very sorry, Jennie."

Jennie laughed and said, "It's okay. Remember, I was the first one to fall asleep on this trip. Still, I did wonder what kind of a vacation this was going to be if you have to hide from me all the time we are alone."

"I wasn't hiding, just pooped. But you're going to have to be more careful with your cuddling on our boat rides or we don't stand a chance of keeping our trip platonic," I answered, thinking, *not that I want it to be that way.*

Jennie and I sat on her bed, talking about Sterling and all the high jinks that went on at the milk barn over the years. She asked about Virginia and the boys who worked with my dad. We had been sitting there for some time with Jennie exaggeratingly avoiding getting to close or touching.

Finally she said, "Well, I guess it's time that you allowed a girl some privacy to change into her night clothes."

I went to my room, thinking, *this is going to be a tough vacation, but I guess I set myself up for this.* A little while later I notice a flickering light under the door.

Fearing fire, I shouted, "Is everything all right out there, Jennie?"

"I think so, but you had better come look," she answered with kind of a laugh.

As I rushed out, there on Jennie's bed sat this beautiful woman wearing a black negligee with a candle burning near a bottle of wine on a table by her bed. I was thunder struck.

I just kept muttering "Oh my God, oh my God."

Jennie smiled and said, "We are not in church and you aren't seeing an angel here, are you?"

"Jennie, Jennie, you must understand, my mind has been seeing the pretty little Jennie from Sterling, not this astonishing beauty I see before me now,"

I stammered as I took her hand and fell to my knees beside the bed.

Jennie's smile broadened. With her face close to mine, she said, "Does that mean you'll marry me, Caleb Carney?"

"Jennie, Jennie, Jennie don't you know that I would say anything, do anything right now, just to be able to ravish you. Don't make me answer a question like that now," I pleaded.

She pulled me to her and we made love until we were both too exhausted to carry on, finally falling to sleep in each other's arms. I woke to the smell of coffee and the morning sun shining in the windows.

"Well, sleepyhead, do you intend to spend your whole week in bed?" Jennie said as she brought me a cup of coffee.

"Not alone I hope," I answered, giving her a kiss.

She cuffed me one and said, "Drink your coffee and let's get going. We can grab breakfast on the way, I saw a sign down at the lake about a fishing trip and I think that might be fun."

The rest of the week we spent most of our days on the lake. There was even a boat that had an evening dinner cruise. We went on that most of the nights we were there. It was a whirlwind of a week. No other life existed but the lake, the cabin, and Jennie and I making love night after night. I couldn't face it ever ending, but end it did.

One morning after waking to the smell of coffee Jennie held me tight as she put my coffee down and said, "This is it, Caleb. We have to get you back to the airport by noon or Earl will leave without you."

My mind screamed, *let him, let him,* but I knew better. We had no way to finance going on like this forever, so thoughts of the real world rushed back in. I wanted to cry out with almost the same anguish that I felt searching the why of losing Josh during those two days I spent on the mountain.

Jennie rocked me gently and said, "We're adults now. Let's not spoil this trip because we have to face the reality of the world. No matter what happens from now on, we will always have this week to dream about. The truth is, it is my hope that we can build on this dream even when we are not together. I know my little marriage proposal the other night was a shock to you, but remember even you talked about marrying before, much to my surprise. My hope is that this trip will make it a more significant thought in your mind. Don't let me scare you. I know we both have a ways to go before marriage would make any sense. Still, it is the one thought that has kept me tied to memories about us since I left Sterling."

"You know that I could never forget this week, and despite all my misgivings about commitment, I have never been this close to anyone else," I said. "Still, I can only promise you that whatever I decide on in that vein, you'll be the first to know. I have two more years of college, and after that I'm not sure what I'll be doing. Hopefully I can find a way to use my education in some profession. I know that life together couldn't always be like this week, but it is a dream worth fighting for."

We put our gear together and left in the car.

We stopped at the first diner to eat and were eerily quiet most of the way back to the airport. When we got there Earl was already rolling out the plane.

Jennie said, "Kiss me quick and walk away without looking back, just like in the World War II movies. I don't want to have you see my tears."

I kissed Jennie, grabbed my gear, and ran toward the plane.

Earl shouted, "Just in time, Caleb. I wasn't sure you would leave her. I'm sure I wouldn't have wanted to."

"I sure didn't want to," I answered just before he fired up the plane. "I know I wouldn't be here if we could have figured out a way to finance that lifestyle for the next sixty years."

Earl didn't seem inclined to talk after we got off the ground. I was happy about that because I was drained. My mind was whirling with all that had happened and been said. One thing I was certain of, my emotions this week had gone way beyond just the sexual part. If this was love then it was wonderful and scary at the same time. I kept remembering part of one of Josh's poems.

Like a fleeting cloud that dissipates
Leaving a vast and empty blue
It pictures the chasm, of my heart
Abysmal life, without you.

By the time we were circling the airfield near Lotus, I knew I had to get a better grip on my thoughts and be ready to face real life again, knowing that Jennie never again would be far from my thoughts. When we landed, Shaq,

Etta, and Etta's intended were there to take me back to Harry and Eunice's.

"Surprise, Caleb," Shaq said, as he introduced me to Avery, Etta's intended. "Harry called and asked if we could pick you up. Seems he had to check something on one of his jobs."

Etta gave me a friendly little kiss and asked, "How did you find Jennie? I bet you two had a lot of catching up to do after spending two years apart. I really miss not be able to spend time in Sterling like I used to with all your family and friends."

"Jennie is fine," I answered, marveling that Etta wasn't creating the same crazy desire in me that she usually did. "I know what you mean about Sterling. I haven't been back much myself in the last two years, except for a few days here and there."

"We have to hurry, Caleb," Shaq said. "I promised to get these two lovebirds back in time for a movie they want to see. I told them it would be tight timing but Etta insisted she wanted to see you. You all can talk in the car."

They all rushed off after dropping me at Eunice's. As they drove away I thought *there goes another part of my life, at least Etta's part in it.* Somehow, in someway it was like the release of a great longing and it felt good.

The next two years of my life could be described as long and lonely. I did work at home one summer because Bruce finally went to work in a garage, like he always wanted to, and I took his place until we could find someone Norman wanted to work with. Harry only had one job going that summer, so he didn't miss me.

Jennie was able to get home for a week. We sure didn't have the privacy that we had at the lake. And, she said, we were too old to be sneaking behind the library anymore and there was no way she was going to the grove with me. Still, it was the best week I had lived since we had been at the lake.

The next year Earl was able to get me back up to New York to see Jennie, but it was only for a day or so and twice I had to cut classes to go with him. Though Jennie had wheels she couldn't always get time off, so I ended up staying at Jolene's farm sometimes—not as romantic but at least we got to see each other.

College finally came to an end. Aaron and Emma brought Mother up for graduation and Eunice and Harry had a big celebration at their house. Shaq brought Loraine and some of the men I used to work with came.

Jennie couldn't make it, but Etta showed up and when she left she kissed me passionately and said, "Jennie asked me to give you this for her."

After catching my breath I said, "I'll be sure to write and thank her for that."

Etta laughed as she left. "I bet you will, Caleb, I bet you will"

Harry had asked if I could work for him at least a month that summer, training some new guy. I had spent a lot of time with him and Eunice and never had to pay room or board, so I felt obligated to stay.

After the party had petered out little Harry, who wasn't so little anymore, and I were in my room talking. "Uncle Caleb," he said, "what are you going to do now that you are out of college?"

"I don't really know just yet, but I guess I'll have to try and find a job in the field of writing."

Just as Eunice called for Hank, he said, "That's pretty scary for you, huh, Uncle Caleb?"

Later that night, just before I went to sleep, I thought Hank must be like Nellie in sensing things.

Because, I was pretty scared at what the world held for me now.

Chapter 2

Training Harry's new men was a snap. The young men he had hired were of Indian ancestry and were already familiar with steel structure work. After three weeks I wasn't really needed, so I applied for a couple of the jobs that Eunice had seen advertised. They were ads for applicants who had writing ability. My first meeting lasted only ten minutes and I could tell by the attitude of the man doing the interview that he thought I was wasting his time. At the second company, my interviewer was a woman who had a much kinder veneer.

After the interview she said, "Mr. Carney, I'm not sure you have the experience or training we are looking for, but I will keep you on the list of potentials."

I thanked her and was about to leave when she said, "If you wouldn't be offended, I could offer you some advice."

I laughed nervously and said, "This is only my second interview and it looks like I could use some."

"Don't take this too hard. Everyone has trouble at first. The first thing you have to do is come better prepared, and you need to act more sure of yourself. Second, you should understand that you need experience. Your best bet would be to look into some small town newspapers, which is where most writers get their start. From there you can submit articles to magazines and periodicals to help get your name out there. When you are successful you can use that in your résumé to apply for a better position. One other thing; the G.I. bill has produced so many college graduates with worldwide experience, employers have a big pool to pick from, so interviewees are going to have to be at the top of their game in order to get started in most any field."

After thanking her again I left, wondering if maybe she had just given me the excuse I needed to get back to Sterling where I belonged. I talked to Eunice and Harry about what had happened. Harry thought there was some truth to what I had been told, but Eunice wanted me to try a couple of other places she had found advertised. One I called said to send my résumé and they would try to get back to me. At the other office I was bluntly told I wasn't right for the job.

I wasn't terribly disappointed about not getting any of these jobs. Staying in Oklahoma hadn't appeal to me anyway. That night in my room, while mulling over my job-hunting results, what really hurt was my seemingly foolish idea that my education was going to easily open doors for me. So much for that old chestnut! Feeling down and lonely in need of a shoulder, I sat down and wrote Jennie.

> *Dear Jennie,*
>
> *Graduation would have been so much better if you had been able to be there; now that I'm out of college we are going to have to find some way to shorten the distance between us. Mother, Aaron, and Emma made it to my graduation. So did Shaq, Lorraine, and Etta, but they couldn't stay long at the party afterward. Etta said to say hi when I wrote or saw you; she was ecstatic to see my mother and sister again and asked if the whole family could possibly come to her wedding this fall.*
>
> *It has been such a long time since Tupper Lake; sometimes I'm afraid I going to wake up and find out it was only a dream.*

I completed training the men for Harry's jobs and applied for a couple of writing positions in Lotus. So far it has been devastating. Seems my education needs a lot of seasoning before I am material for most writing jobs, at least the ones in the cities. In fact, one manager even told me that I probably should try getting a job at some small town newspaper until I had more experience; too bad Sterling doesn't have a newspaper. I'm not sure what my next move will be. I am going to be meeting with Jake, who did land a good job last year in Lotus at a paper he had been writing for while he was still in college. Jake had worked at a paper in Oscin back when he was still in high school; he always was one step ahead of most of the class when it came to writing.

Even though you can't feel my tears wetting you blouse, writing you helps clear my mind. Still, even thinking of you raises wants, not just sexual, but also the want of your loving embrace.

With the hope our thoughts are still entwined,
Caleb

Jake was able to get me a job in the copy room of the paper he worked for. It wasn't a job writing; it was mostly just formulating someone else's writing so that the article fit the pages. Jake pointed out that at least it was at a newspaper and it was a start and that I could learn a lot about how a newspaper works from a job like that. He was right about that. I got to see the type of articles that were being accepted by the editor as I positioned them to fit the newspaper pages. Though some of the writings interested me I could only scan them at work and had to read the paper later if I wanted to fully understand them. The more I studied newspapers the surer I was that I wouldn't enjoy this type of writing as a way to make a living. Since the job didn't excite me life became rather dull. Earl hadn't been making any trips up north so I couldn't get to see Jennie.

Mother, Aaron, and Emma came up for Etta's wedding. I had expected some kind of an Indian ceremony but it turned out to be more conventional.

When I first heard about her getting married I imagined the pain of having to watch her walk down the isle. Like always, Etta took every red-blooded man's breath away as she walked down the aisle. Still, I didn't feel the kind of pain I had envisioned, though it sure brought our walk on the mountain back to mind.

My mother and Etta's mother got together at the reception and called me over.

Mother said, "Caleb, you never told us that you were such a hero up here. To hear Etta's mother tell it you cast some kind of a spell over Etta that restored her sanity."

"Oh no, Mother, it wasn't anything like that," I answered. "When I first met Etta she was already getting over her teenage rebellious stage. It's just that I met her through Shaq at the same time, and as you well know Etta's the one who cast spells, not me."

I spotted Shaq and quickly moved away from the mothers, hoping to quell that kind of talk.

When I asked him about the Indian side of this event, he laughed and said, "You know, Caleb, we aren't full-blooded Indians. Still, Avery and Etta have agreed to renew their vows Indian style at the reservation, just to please my uncles. I might be able to get you an invite if you're really interested."

I got a chance to dance with Etta just before Aaron announced that the Carney family had to leave for their long drive back to Sterling.

As we danced, Etta said, "I really love Avery and we are a good match, but I have to tell you that it was very much on my mind before, that I really could have become a Carney if we had a chance. Maybe you should thank your lucky stars that I met Avery."

"I'm not sure about my lucky stars, Etta, but I am pleased that you have found someone who makes you happy," I answered, cringing at the thoughts she had provoked.

As we finished the dance Etta said, "Promise me that I will at least get an invite when your big day comes. From what I have heard it's going to be Jennie who ends your harem lifestyle."

As the music ended I said, "I can't promise you it's going to be Jennie but I do promise to invite you."

Etta started walking away but then turned back and, looking me in the eye, said, "Caleb, don't hold on to the past so tight that it destroys the future. Now that's a quote from a wonderful person who my brother Shaq brought to me once, when I was lost."

Aaron was motioning to me as Etta walked away, wanting me to say my good-byes to Mother and my sister so they could get on their way. I walked out with them and said, "I guess it's near time for me go too."

"I bet seeing Etta married was one of the hardest things you have ever done, huh, Caleb," Emma teased as she kissed me good-bye.

Aaron and I had had a very in-depth talk about my job situation before. He was adamant in telling me that in the end I would see the gain from my college education. He reminded me again as we said goodbye.

"Someday soon I hope you'll will be telling me I'm right, so hang in there," he said.

I kissed Mother and thanked Aaron for his input. I knew that they would have to stop at Eunice's to say good-bye and pick up their things there, but I didn't feel like another sad goodbye scene, so I went to nearby a bar and ordered a beer.

Sat there in kind of a dark mood when someone said, "I'll be damned, it must be my forte in life. Damned if you don't still look just like one of Etta's castoffs."

I turned and there was June. Seems she had graduated from the dance hall bar to working this one. "I'll be off in about twenty minutes. Want some company? You sure look like you could use some cheering up."

I'm not sure what happened after June came back. I wasn't used to drinking much beer and I remember starting to feel it. The next real conscious thing I remember was June waking me and handing me a cup of coffee.

"You had better pull it together, Caleb," she said. "Its daylight and by this time someone somewhere is probably really worried about you."

After drinking her coffee and realizing what must have happened, I wasn't in a mood to find out for sure. So I called Eunice and told her I was all right, just celebrated a little too much and slept it off at a friend's house.

I vaguely remembered June saying something about being married and divorced so I asked, "Are we all right, June? I seem to have lost most of the night somehow."

June gave me a big hug and said, "We're all right, and you needn't worry about June. She's used to picking up scraps from other people's tables."

"Damn! June, talk like that isn't going to relieve my mind. I don't want anyone feeling like I was using them," I answered, still feeling a little woozy

"Here, take your things and leave. If anyone did any using last night it was me, not you," she said as she opened the door for me.

"One thing more," she shouted as I was going down the steps. "You should learn how to hold your beer better or give up drinking it."

It took a couple of weeks after the wedding for me to expunge the ill feeling that night had left me with. I was still tormented by the thought that the right thing to do was to go back and see June again. I settled by writing about my tears to Jennie, but of course not about June. I could justify this because Jennie and I had been writing each other yearning letters every couple of weeks. About six months after I went to work at Jake's paper, I received this letter from Jennie:

> *My Dear Caleb,*
>
> *I have had some discussions with the Jolenes about our desire to be reunited and that they should be thinking about replacing me. As you know, they have treated me like family and were very upset about possibly losing me but said they fully understood that I wasn't a little girl anymore. A week or so after that, Mr. Jolene came to me with a proposition. He said he had contacts with most all the newspapers up here and was sure he could get you hired if you were interested. If you are, send your résumé and he will do the rest.*
>
> *Caleb, I know that this might put you in a bind right now, but please give it serious consideration. He said the pay wouldn't be the greatest but if I keep this job we surely would have enough income to support a household. My mind says this needs careful consideration but my heart says, "Grab it, grab it, please, please grab it." Then when my mind brings me back to where our living for the moment has lead us, I cry, "Be still, wild heart, be still."*
>
> *I know this letter is short and it contains a strong confused message but it carries my tears to your shoulders and my heart needs an answer.*

Your angel from Tupper Lake,
  Jennie

I was beginning to see the job that Jake had got me was going nowhere, but when I talked to Jake about leaving he said, "I thought you understood that you are under contract here for a year. If you leave before then it'll always be a black mark against you in your job searches. If you have to leave I would advise you to wait until your year is up. I know that they don't expect much more than that from anyone in your job, so if you wait until then, you will be leaving on good terms."

After discussing my situation with Harry and my sister I decided Jake was right and I had better work out my contract. As much as I wanted to be with Jennie, it seemed much better to make a move like that in July rather than in the middle of the winter.

My Dearest Jennie,
  It seems that I am under contract for a year on the job I have now. Though I could break the contract, I have been informed that if I did that it could interfere with job searches throughout my life. So far, what I've seen of the newspaper business causes me to believe I have chosen the wrong profession. Harry and Eunice have some experience with résumés when they are hiring and have cautioned me that the last thing I want is a black mark on mine. What I'm trying to say through the heartache and tears is that I will have to refuse Mister Jolene's offer, at least for now.
  It would be kinder of you to not sign off with a mention of Tupper Lake. How is a man supposed to think straight and make intelligent decisions if his mind is on cloud nine? Earl is flying into an airport close to Oscin, so I have arranged a few days off so I can go see my family next week. He told me he thinks he will be going up your way again in a couple of weeks but it is only for a day or so. As soon as he knows for sure I'll let you know. I am able to swap days off with one of the men who

*work at my job at the paper so it will be okay since it is only for
a day or so. I can't wait to see you.*

> *Until that sweet day,*
> *Caleb*

Homer was at the airport outside of Oscin when we landed. Boy, was he excited about watching us land.

I introduced him to Earl, who laughed at his excitement and said, "Homer, you should have been there the first time Caleb landed with me. He had his eyes closed and I thought he was going to rip the seat out of the plane. I do believe that if there was any other way he could see his sweet Jennie he never would have flown again."

"I think I might be a little scared too, but I sure would love to ride in a plane like that," Homer said.

"Tell you what. I have to be out of here three days from now by one p.m. If you come an hour earlier than that and I can get permission from the gurus who run this port, I'll take you for a little ride."

As we left the airport Homer said, "Can we do that, Caleb, come back early so I can fly with Earl?"

"I don't see why not. You deserve that much for carting me around when I come home," I answered, thinking what a good guy that Earl was.

"I almost forgot, Caleb. Emma and Aaron have set a date of the thirty-first of July for their wedding. Hester and Richard are coming back from Japan the second week of July so they can be at the wedding. Aaron insists that they get married at the farm like Richard and Hester did. He says we should all get married there, and that it would make a great story to pass on to our grandchildren. How about you? I hear that things have become pretty serious between you and Jennie. Are you planning on having your wedding at the farm?" he asked

"Wow! What are you trying to do, marry off all your brothers and sisters at once? I know you've always had a soft spot in your heart about Jennie and it's true that we've become closer, if not in space at least in thought. Still, the truth is, though we have mentioned marriage it has only been in passing," I answered, thinking again of Tupper Lake and Jennie's 'Will you marry me, Caleb?'

It was great being back with the family but the days passed much too fast. I checked in with Joan's parents but Joan was gone for the week. During the conversation with her father he hinted that she was away with a boyfriend. Joan and I hadn't been able to spend much time together since my second year of college but she had written. In several of her letters she had mentioned growing beyond childhood's wanting dreams, though she always hoped to retain her fond memories.

I had answered: *They say that childhood is preparation for adulthood but I wasn't sure I had become to adult yet, because of the pain and sorrow I felt about my dissipating harem.*

The truth about Joan still eludes me somehow. My thoughts about her have always been a mixture of want and fear. I have sometimes thought it might have been better for both of us if I had succumbed to her untamed sexual advances when we were up on Mount Fay.

While home, I had a long talk with Dad. "I don't know if I ever expressed how proud I have been about the way you handled things while I was laid up," he said. "Finding Norman and Bruce was the key that made everything work out. Even now with Bruce gone, their friend Vance, who took his place, has worked out well, maybe even better since Vance doesn't squabble with Norman like Bruce used to."

"I'm happy that things worked out for you, but remember, I didn't find those boys," I answered. "From the get-go, Norman did the pushing, first for him, then for Bruce, to work for us. I know that Norman made what could have been a trying time in my life into a time I will always treasure. As for their squabbles, once you understood that they were brothers who truly loved and needed each other the arguing became part of their grandeur." I smiled as I thought about my year with those boys.

The night before it was time to leave a row started about who could go to see Homer getting his first airplane ride.

Emma said, "Look, let me call Aaron and if he can get free everyone can go, if we take two cars."

The next day the whole Carney clan left the farm before ten in the morning for the trip to the airport. The night before I had spent some time alone with Aaron and Emma. I marveled at the fact that they had been engaged for so long without getting married.

Aaron said, "Oh, it has been terribly hard, Caleb, but remember how I told you my education was paid for by the company I worked for? Well, as soon as I finished my degree they started shipping me all over the world on some of their projects. We were lucky that your mother allowed Emma to come to California for about two weeks last year when I was stuck there. We are so excited now that we can finally be married in only a few more months."

It was hard for me to believe as much as I wanted to that my sister Emma has stayed chaste all this time, considering my history with girls. Somehow I fell asleep with that not being much of a burden for me. After all, Emma at over twenty-five was no little girl anymore.

The whole family ended up at the airport to watch Homer's first airplane ride. Earl put on quite a show. He even did a loop and a roll before coming back in for a landing.

I heard Mother take in her breath and Dad say, "I hope he knows what he's doing."

"Now don't get worried. Earl has been flying that plane so long it's like a part of him. You should see some of the cow pasture airports he lands and takes off from," I said, trying to sound reassuring.

There was great excitement throughout my family as Homer returned and I got ready to leave.

"That's some brother you have there," Earl said. "I've had people faint or throw up during that maneuver, but your brother just hollered 'Can we do it again?' "

"Yeah," I said. "He's the brave one all right. Why, he had a kissing club with most of the girls in town at a time in his life when other boys his age were just dreaming of doing things like that."

It was the end of February before Earl called to say he was headed to northern New York. When I met him at the little airport I noticed his plane was fitted with skis. It was only the thoughts of holding Jennie again that gave me the courage to continue the trip. Earl didn't even mention the skis as we took off. I suppose he had been using them all winter and hadn't given my fears a thought.

When we came to the airstrip in New York, he did say, "You had better buckle up tight. Sometimes I kind of bounce landing with skis in snow like this."

Though I closed my eyes and held on tight I didn't notice that landing was much difference from any of his other landings.

Jennie was there waiting with some guy in a uniform. I had a kind of misgiving about that but it turned out it was George Jolene, the one who owned the car we always used. He was home for a month between assignments.

After the introductions he said, "You don't need to worry. I told Jennie she can use the car while you are here. I can always grab a farm vehicle if I need transportation. Jennie was hesitant about driving up here in the snow so I drove for her. Besides, I wanted to see who this writer was that flew into cow pastures just to see our little Jennie."

I laughed and said, "I appreciate your coming, George, because if she got stuck on the way and wasn't here when I landed, I might of had a heart attack or something."

On the way back to the Jolene's, we had great conversations about George being in the service. He knew about Josh and asked if there was some kind of memorial in our hometown for him. I told him about the ball field named after him and about the flagpole and garden with the plaque dedicated to his memory.

Jennie noticing the effect talking about Josh was having on me, and so broke in. "Hey, did you come up to hash over war experiences or to see me?" she asked.

"I'm sorry, Jennie," George said with a laugh. "I know you two only have one day, and I promise I'll disappear as soon as we get back to the farm."

How fast a day can go. Jennie didn't want to go to a motel the night I was there, fearing it might upset the Jolenes', so we had to settle for a lot less then I had anticipated. I spoke to Mr. Jolene about the prospects around there.

He was very honest, saying, "The truth is, money wise things aren't the greatest but we do have a couple of old-time editors who could be a great help to someone like you just starting out."

I told him I would have a decision soon and would send him my résumé if I decided to go that route. The next day it started snowing some so Jennie asked George if he could come to the airport with us, in case the driving got bad on the way back. All in all it was kind of an uneventful trip. Taking off and landing on skis turned out to be the trip's highlights, especially the bouncing landing we made just as it was turning dark when we got back. Even Earl looked a little shaken that time.

"Whew," he said. "We'll have to start watching our time a little better on these winter trips so we won't be caught landing in the dark."

As it turned out there were no more winter trips, at least not to New York. I sent Jennie my résumés, telling her that I wouldn't be able to be up there before sometime in August, because I wanted to go to Emma's wedding and spend some time in Sterling before committing to anything.

I resigned my job in Lotus on July 7 and took a train for Sterling the next day. About a week after I got home I received a call from Joan. She asked me if we could go see a movie. Thinking that would be nice, I set a date up for the following night. When I picked her up she was in a bubbly mood and her kisses were definitely on the passionate side. The movie she had picked out was a rather convoluted coming-of-age story that had a pretty depressing ending.

We were both rather quiet on the way home, but as we entered Sterling Joan said, "Caleb, do we have time to go set at the swings for a while?"

"Sure, Joan, just like old times. Only this time it will be a much older Joan and Caleb," I answered, wondering what was on her mind. Surprisingly, we still fit into the swing seats and we sat there swinging slowly for a long time, saying nothing.

When the town clock struck one she said, "I guess we had better go, but I need to ask you one more thing first. I will be in Sterling only a couple of more days and I would like to walk the mountain with you one more time. I hope it won't be the last time, but life is fleeting and one can never tell."

Thinking about Etta's warning, about not holding on to the past too tight, I said, "If that's what my little ice-cream girl wants to do, then let's do it, say ten o'clock tomorrow morning."

I picked up Joan the next morning and we drove to the foot of the mountain and started hiking. We visited all my old haunts, and then after climbing the fire tower we started our run down the mountain. Halfway down Joan stopped and said, "I have to ask you a big, big favor. If you want to say no I'll understand."

Joan just stood there, kind of quivering like she did whenever I held her after she had been raped over five years ago. Wanting to help her, I said,

"We've been sharing secrets since our first ice-cream date, so don't be afraid no matter what you need to ask."

Taking a deep breath she said, "Caleb, I want to make love with you. Excepting that time I was taken advantage of, which I don't remember, I have never had sex." I guess I must have winced or drawn in my breath because she continued, "It's not what you think. I'm not asking for any commitment. It's just sometimes when I'm with my boyfriend I feel like I might want to do it. One thing for sure, he does. What really scares me is I'm not sure what will happen. I might panic or start screaming or something. I have given this a lot of thought and I have decided that if we did it, no matter what happened you would understand and help me through it. I hope I am not asking to much, Caleb, but I really need you to help me."

There was no doubt that Joan was sexually attractive. She was a pretty and a very desirable girl, but I had made such a practice of keeping these feelings out of our relationship that I was taken back by all of this. Joan stood looking at me, still quivering, with tears welling in her eyes. I took her hand and gently led her back into the woods; the very excitement about the situation was more then any red-blooded man needed.

Still, I murmured, "Last chance, Joan. Are you sure?"

Joan grabbed me, kissed me, and said, "Thank you, Caleb, thank you."

I started out being tentative but soon found myself having sex with a wildly aggressive woman. After as we both lay sated on the forest floor, I asked Joan if she was okay.

She said, "Harem or no harem, where in the world would I find anyone as understanding as you."

I laughed and said, "I'm not really a loser in this little game, Joan. Today was a culmination of all the desires that you have caused in me over the years."

As we got up Joan gave me a little kiss and said, "Was once really enough?"

"Maybe not, but we have other obligations and I think it would be better for you if you took some time to think today over," I answered, thinking we better get out of here before I change my mind. Joan kept giving me little hugs as we walked down the mountain; she reminded me of a kid who had just received a new toy.

At the foot of the mountain Joan said, "Caleb, there is one more thing. Despite your nickname of *Beverly's Virgin*, none of us really believed that as a barn boy, you could have been that virtuous. What I need to know is how do I rate on your list?"

Her 'a barn-boy shit' really hit home and started angering me. Boy, I guess Homer had her right. Still not wanting to erase the joy in her eyes, I answered, "If, and I do mean if, I had such a list I'm sure you would rank right near the top."

When we arrived at Joan's house she held me close and said, "Caleb, you can't know how much you have done for your little ice-cream girl today. You even have me wondering what it would have been like if things had been different last time."

I didn't really know how to respond. Still, I said, "You should remember that there has always been a deep emotion between us and that makes today so much different. Now you have to stop enticing me and let me go. I'm already over an hour late from the time I was supposed to meet Homer."

"Okay, okay," she said. "I'll let you go but I can be here only two more days and you have to promise we can get together at least one more time."

I left Joan without actually making a commitment and arrived home to find Homer had left without me. He had asked me to go with him to look at a car he was thinking of buying.

When he came back I apologized for being late. "No big deal," he said. "I knew I wasn't interested the minute I heard it run."

The rest of my time in Sterling went way too fast. Though Joan left a call for me I had decided we were better of having our memories end with our mountain episode, if indeed they were going to end. Aaron and Emma's wedding at the farm was a lot of fun. Harry and Eunice had come down and Hester and Richard were back from Japan. For the first time in a long time the Carney family was all together, of course with the exception of Josh. We had a grand celebration, which I'm sure the Carneys and the town will remember for some time. Aaron and Emma were leaving for Pennsylvania the next day. His company had a big office there and this was going to be his permanent assignment.

Aaron and Emma had decided to stay at the farm in Emma's room that night, so Jason and Francis had snuck up to her room and tied a cowbell and some sleigh bells to the springs under the bed. I think Aaron was too smart to get caught in anything like that because the next day we found the bells back in the barn. I had two weeks more in Sterling before I had to leave for New York. I spent much of my time with my brothers roaming the haunts of town and going fishing. It seemed strange that Nellie was the only sister left home. She and I spent one morning roaming around Mount Fay. After getting beat by Nellie in our race down the mountain, she said with a laugh, "Growing old, huh, Caleb?

"Not too old that I can't spank your butt if you pick on me like that," I answered.

"Seriously though," she said. "I still sense an ambivalence in you about life. Are we still fighting leaving childhood after all these years? I would think your commitment to move to New York with Jennie would have settled most of those issues for you. While you are away I have such high hopes, but I'm not with you for long before I sense something different."

"Nellie, you have to stop scaring your big brother by trying to analyze him like that. I have met with some disappointments since I left college but I guess that's to be expected."

"Are you sure it isn't more then that?" she asked. "I sure was catching some vibes the day you came back from being with Joan."

"It was really nothing to worry about," I answered, thinking, *God help the boy who falls in love with Nellie.* "Joan and I have been holding hands since we were little kids and she is moving on in her life. It was like a parting of ways or a good-bye to childhood thing. Sure it was emotional, but it certainly wasn't so earth shaking that it should upset my little sister."

Thinking, *Lord knows how long it will be before I see Sterling again,* I spent my last couple of evenings with Mother and Dad and the family and all too soon Homer was dropping me off at the bus station and I was climbing on a bus that again was carrying me away from Sterling.

Chapter 3

Jennie met me after I arrived in Inchoate at the bus station, and we sat in the car just holding each other without talking. Somehow I finally knew that in her arms was where I belonged beyond all my doubts, despite the other girls who had been in my life, even if it meant I might be leaving Sterling forever. Here, I was supplied with the reassurances that were so missing in my life. Here was the same warmth, strength, and understanding that had rescued me from the dark pit of desolation that came over me when we lost Josh.

Jennie broke me from my reverie with a passionate kiss, and said, "Caleb, we have to do some planning. Let's find a quiet restaurant where we can discuss things over dinner."

The town where I was dropped off was a long way from the Jolene farm.

After we found our restaurant Jennie said, "I told the Jolenes that you had college friends in this area and you would probably would like to spend a couple of days here. I didn't want you to have to be making decisions as important as we have to make, while you're influenced by the environment at the farm."

As much as I was pleased to hear we were going to be alone, my mind hadn't grasped the magnitude of the situation that my coming here was putting her in.

Wanting to start out truthfully, I said, "Jennie, my life has been so convoluted that my major plan has been only 'I'm finally going to be staying in Jennie's arms.' Look, you lay it all out on the table and we will deal with it together."

"You big boob, you must have understood that there isn't any way we could shack up together while I'm still working at Jolenes," Jennie said, giving me a whack.

"Well, let's get married then," I answered, much to my own surprise.

Jennie sighed and said, "We should have given all of this more thought. Then we could have arranged to be married somehow before you came up."

I laughed and said, "How would that work? Would we both have proxies? I wouldn't want my proxy spending my wedding night with you."

"I don't know how we could have done it. Maybe arranged a wedding with a justice of peace or someone like that as long as we had all our paperwork ready," she answered just as the waitress was putting down our dinners.

"Let's not spoil our few days here, Jennie," I said. "I can find a place to stay while we arrange some kind of a marriage. Then, if you want, we can do it up in splendor some time later. The last two marriages in my family were held at our farm. Aaron, Emma's husband, said he thinks we all should get married there and make it a Carney tradition." *Wouldn't my brothers have fun with us if that happened*, I thought.

The waitress brought around our deserts and said, "I don't want to butt in but we have a justice of peace in town who has presided over more than one wedding with papers he supplies. They probably wouldn't be the best papers if you happened to have a court case, like a divorce or a will or something. Still, in ordinary circumstances they will stand up and like the man says, you can always do it in splendor later. Let me know if I can help."

Jennie and I just sat looking at each other for a few minutes and almost together we said, "Why not?"

We called the waitress over and asked what it would cost and how could we set it up. She said, "For you two I'll get you a bargain. Fifty dollars and it's a done deal."

I said, "Okay, but we pay after it's a done deal, not before."

"Give me your names and birth dates and meet me here tomorrow at nine o'clock sharp. You can get married right here in the back room."

After we left the restaurant we found a cabin just outside of town. As soon as we were settled I said, "Jennie, I'm all for it, but I don't want to do it if it bothers you."

Jennie was quiet for a few moments. Then she said, "As long as I'm sure that you will consider this as binding as a real wedding, I want to do it. I want you to know first what that means. You and all that you are belong to me, not as my slave but as my lover and to me only. I need that kind of promise from you if we are going through with this."

"Jennie," I said, thinking about how I felt back in the car. "I may never be able to promise you wealth and fame but I can promise you that my heart will always belong to you, and only you."

"I'm asking for a little more then just your heart, Caleb. I need to know if I'm going to be your wife, that from now on I will be your one and only, regardless of what kind of papers we have."

"I'm going to borrow something from Josh. I feel like he must have written it just for us, at this moment." Then I recited part of Josh's poem, "My Love," wishing I could remember all of it.

Do not think that I will ever leave
Or that my love is make believe
Have no fears and show no sorrow
My love will last beyond the morrow.

We made love most of the night, getting up early so we could be at the restaurant at nine. It was almost like Jennie had planned this because she dressed in the prettiest dress I had ever seen her in. Luckily I had a sports jacket that wasn't too wrinkled. We arrived at the restaurant a little before nine. At first we thought we had been tricked but soon the waitress showed up with an elderly couple in tow. The justice showed us the papers to make sure he had the names right and much to our surprise followed that with a by-the-book wedding procedure. It was authentic right down to the "You may kiss the bride" part. I don't think we would have felt any more married even if we had been in a big church.

The waitress went out and came back in carrying a little cake with a bride and groom on it that she had fashioned out of toothpicks and pipe cleaners. There seemed to be tears in her eyes when she presented it. We paid the justice the fifty dollars and his wife asked if we could afford it.

Jennie said, "It won't be a problem for us," as she tried to give the waitress an extra ten.

The waitress refused, "No! No!" and ran from the room.

Jennie started after her but the justice's wife said, "No, leave her be. Let me tell you about her. Her sweetheart was going to be shipped overseas during World War II and he tried to get her to have a quickie wedding before he left. She said no. He was killed in Normandy and she's been working in that restaurant ever since and every once in a while she brings couples like you to us. I know that marrying people without all the papers might seem kind of shady and we did too at first. Loretta, that's the girl who brought us to you, convinced us that it was the right thing in the cases like yours. Your wedding is only the third time we have done this. I can assure you that with the exception of a severe court examination, your papers will stand up. Besides, I bet most people who have been married a few years couldn't produce any papers anyhow."

Again we thanked the justice and went looking for a different place to have breakfast, as the restaurant we were in served only lunch and dinner. After eating we walked around the town.

As we were going by a jewelry store Jennie said, "Let's go in and see if we can afford some wedding bands."

The store didn't have anything we felt we should spend that much on, so we told them we would have to think about it and get back to them. Later, as we were walking down a side street, I spotted a pillow that had two hearts marked "his" and "hers" embroidered on it with a bow that bound them together.

I said, "Let's buy it, Jennie. It will be a memento of our wedding day."

While getting the pillow Jennie noticed a counter that held hundreds of rings. Searching through them we found several good wedding bands. There were several that fit Jennie but the only one that fit me had an unreadable inscription on the inside. Jennie found that vexing. The man behind the counter looked at it and took it into a back room.

46

He returned in a few minutes, handed us the ring, and said, "How's that now?"

Jennie was pleased with how he had removed the inscription, so now each of us had a ring. After paying for our purchases I started to put the ring on.

Jennie said, "No, not now, Caleb, not now."

Tired of walking around the town we took in an afternoon showing at the local movie theater and then went back to where Loretta worked to have our dinner. We tried to thank her again and she cautioned us not to talk about it and to allow her happiness for us to be her thanks.

Back at the cabin Jennie said, "I propose we have a little ceremony of the rings as we put them on. I'll give you a few minutes to compose what you would like to say, while I get ready."

"I might need more then a few minutes. You shouldn't surprise me like that," I said.

She laughed and replied, "Aren't you supposed to be a writer? Isn't composing what you have to do?"

A few minutes later she came out dressed in the same black negligee she wore on our first night at Tupper Lake.

Taking my hand she said, "Caleb, with this ring I am placing myself in your loving care for the rest of my life and I promise to love you and honor the title, Caleb's wife, in everything I do forever more."

Then she held out her hand.

She was so gorgeous standing there that my voice shook as I slid on her ring and said, "Jennie, my love for you will be as continuous as this ring and purer then the gold it is made out of, and the honor of hearing 'That's Jennie, Caleb's wife,' will forever be mine."

We fell into each other's arms until our kissing became too passionate to resist as we spent our first night as husband in wife making deep, passionate love.

We had discovered that Inchoate wasn't too far from Tupper Lake so we left early the next morning, deciding to spend our last day and night there. We went fishing on one of the boats and that night took a dinner cruise. We were even lucky enough to get the same cabin we had the last time we were there. The next morning bright and early we were on the road to Jolenes' farm, coordinating our wedding story to kill any suspicion our being married might cause.

Mrs. Jolene met us at the door when we arrived at the farm. Jennie proudly showed her our rings.

She gave Jennie a big hug and said, "Everyone here was just waiting for Caleb to show up so we could go to your wedding. We will miss doing that but at least we can throw you a party, Jolene style. That is, if Caleb and you wouldn't mind."

"We would be very pleased to have all of you share in our joy, but our immediate concern is finding suitable housing," Jennie said.

Mrs. Jolene broke out in a big smile and said, "We've already anticipated that. As you know, Jennie, we have several properties near the farm that we have acquired over the years. One of them has been vacant for a couple of weeks and Henry and I were thinking you and Caleb might use it. It is fairly well furnished and in move-in condition now if you want it, but of course you welcome to stay at your room for a while if that's what you want. Why don't we go right now to look over the house before you make any decisions?"

The house was about half a mile from the farm. It was small but neat and clean and fully furnished, even up to the bedding on the bed.

I could see Jennie was pleased so I asked, "What is the rent on a place like this up here, Mrs. Jolene?"

"Please, Caleb," she said, "call me Mary. You know Jennie is like family and it makes me feel old hearing that misses all the time, especially with your accent. You don't need worry about the rent. We'll work something out later that will be fair to both of us. Now, what's it going to be, here or at the farm? I have to get back. Without Jennie here to run the milk house I have to keep an eye on things."

Jennie said, "If it is all the same to you, I think Caleb would be more comfortable here." Her perception was just one of the many reasons why I felt like I had made such a wise choice in marrying her.

"Then it's settled and I'm out of here, but I expect Jennie back on the job tomorrow because Henry and I have a little trip of our own planned," Mary said with a wink as she went out the door.

After checking out our new abode we went back to the farm to start moving Jennie's things from the room that had been her home for over five years.

Jennie grew somewhat wistful and said, "Do you remember when you first brought me up here? I was scared but determined that life had to include more for me then just Sterling and a job at Muldons. I became contented here after a while, but it was like something in my life was missing. Ever since Tupper Lake I have known that something was you. Now that you are here with me life is complete."

As happy as I was that Jennie and I now were one, I still did not feel the comfort she conveyed in being so far away from Sterling. Not wanting to break her mood I said. "Being here is all new to me and it will take a while before it seems like home to me, but it means we are finally together and that's the most important thing in my life right now."

We spent a few days getting settled, and then under Henry Jolene's guidance I visited the town papers that were closest to the farm. They were expecting me and it was evident that Henry Jolene had a lot of pull in this area. My résumé didn't include much in the way of writing examples, so at the first paper it was suggested that I write an editorial on the pros and cons of the Marshall Plan that had been initiated by the United States after World War II so they could get an idea of my writing style.

At the second paper, after seeing my history of the work I had been doing at the Lotus paper, they offered me a similar position there with the possibility of eventually becoming the head of that department. Financially, neither paper was offering as much as I was making in Lotus and though I expected that after talking to other people who were working there, I found the chances of a much higher pay were slim.

After discussing it with Henry and Jennie for a couple of days and feeling that going back to what I was doing in the Lotus paper was a dead end, I excepted a position offered at the *Lawrenceville Daily*. They were happy with my editorial but advised me my beat at first would be meetings in small-town government and it was different than writing editorials.

My first assignment was at a selectmen's meeting in Westville, an adjoining town. After introducing myself and making sure I got all their names spelled right, I took notes for the next two hours on what I found to be a very interesting concept of how a small town was run. The next morning I went to the paper and typed up my report. After I had finished I was sent to check on a tractor-trailer accident and the police investigation that had just been called in. When I returned I was informed the editor wanted to see me in his office.

When I entered he said, "Caleb, you seem to have some misconception on what reporting is. You can't write what basically is your opinion of a meeting. It has to be written verbatim. You have to be very careful, especially in these small towns, not to misquote or misinterpret anybody. Now if you took good enough notes to rewrite this that way, I still could use it and I need it on my desk ASAP."

Going back to my notes I quickly found out I had to take more accurate notes but I pieced together a small article about the meeting that the editor at least accepted, even though I knew he wasn't pleased. I worded my report on the accident very carefully so as not to be opinionated. It took several more tries and calls to the wood shed by the editor before I got a story through without revisions.

Life in Lawrenceville wasn't bad for Jennie and me with the exception of my having to be out two or three nights every week to attend meetings my paper wanted covered. Some days Jennie had to be at the farm early and if I had been out the night before I didn't even get to see her on those mornings. Life where I could be with Jennie every night was good and though I didn't see my job as being an end all with its limited areas for advancement, it was a writing job. A few months after Jennie and I married we received a letter from Joan addressed to Mr. and Mrs. Carney. Surprisingly it addressed Jennie.

> *Dear Jennie,*
> *I ran into Homer and he told me about you sneaking off with my ice-cream date and marrying him. Hurray for you and lucky him. I remember when we talked that we wondered if he would ever settle down and ask one of us to marry him. Though Caleb and I held hands all through childhood and beyond I think it has been evident to both of us for some time that we would never survive as a married couple. I envy you in some ways; it is time in our lives to couple up and start families. I have been close to heading down that aisle myself but troubles, mostly mine, have prevented it, but I still have prospects and hope. I know Caleb is with someone who truly cares for him, and that makes me very happy.*

I will not be spending much time in Sterling now that I have found a job I really like in New York City. Please drop me a line once in a while so I can stay abreast of old friends from Sterling.
The Old Maid of the Pack,
Joan

After reading the letter Joan said, "I wondered what had happened with Joan. You haven't spoken much about her in the last few years. I would have thought she would have found someone while she was in college."

"I met with her a couple of times when I was back in Sterling but like she said, we haven't been to close since she started college," I answered, thinking, *I'm glad I didn't meet with her again after that day on the mountain.*

One of the things Jennie and I had agreed on before we got married is that the past was past and we would never let it come between us.

But she did say, "I'll save her address. I think it will be good for all of us who came from Sterling to keep in touch at least a couple of times a year."

"I think that's great. Maybe we should contact more of our friends and tell them we are a happily married couple now," I said, wondering where Joan had met Homer.

He had been trying out different jobs since he graduated from high school, working at Stuarts, at landscaping, and as a plumber's helper. None of these occupations seemed agree with him and he would end up back working for Muldons. When I left he told me that Richard had told him about some opportunities in his company that might interest him. He would have to go to a company school for a while but what excited Homer most was that it was his chance to get out of Sterling and do some traveling. I was happy for him and in a way now even I could see there was some advantage to being away from Sterling. I don't believe that Jennie and I would ever have discovered our true feelings if either one of us had stayed in Sterling.

Mother had expressed some indignation at what Jennie and I had done. Still she and Jason had kept us informed about everything that was happening in the Carney household. Dad had been able to contract only one more job using the horses to stick lumber after finishing the big job they were on when I left. Jocklin won the bid for sawing, cutting, and logging on a five-hundred-acre lot but all the lumber was going to be trucked out green as it was cut. Dad stayed with the marking job and Norman took over as the roller in the mill.

Changing jobs wasn't the hard part; the hard part was having to part with the horses, Roxy and Molly. After having them all those years, neither Dad, Norman, nor any of the family wanted to face the fact that at their age if they sold them they probably would end up as dog meat. There weren't many good options for old horses but they postponed having to make any decisions by retiring them to the farm. Jason even got a little work for them at the Muldon farms, enough at least to help with their keep.

Jason was graduating from high school and had applied to several colleges. Though he was going to have to contribute some by working, the Carney sons-in-law had been contributing to a fund to help with college tuitions. They were all great believers that education was going to be much more important now. It was evident that after World War II the country was developing many new industries, while speeding up and expanding many of the old ones. I know Aaron and Richard always preached that the good-paying jobs would always be in management.

I knew in my job the pay wasn't anything to brag about and there wasn't any way we could live comfortably without Jennie's pay. Unless I put in for a lot of extra night meetings, my pay wouldn't cover much more than our rent and car payments.

When I talked to Jennie about it she would just say, "We're together and comfortable and you just have to keep writing and sending things out. Some day you'll be recognized and your writing will start bringing in the money."

It was hard to think like that, because after a year of working on the paper I had gotten only a couple of articles accepted by any magazine. Even then the pay was a year's subscription or a couple of their books. As exciting as it was to have my writing accepted, it was plain to see it wasn't going to be enough to pay all the bills.

A year after we were married the Jolenes' arranged for a girl to take Jennie's place and I wangled a couple weeks off from the paper and we made plans to spend some time in Sterling with our families. We took our time driving back to Sterling, staying at a cabin at Indian Lake. We had thought about staying at Tupper Lake again but Indian Lake was more of a halfway point. Still, we made it part of our plans to spend a night at Tupper on the way back. I guess we will always have a soft spot in our hearts for Tupper Lake, as that is where our romance first really blossomed.

After we reached the Carney household in Sterling, Mother spent the first half hour we were there chastising us.

She said, "Never in my life would I have believed that the first one of my sons to get married would inform his family weeks after it was already done. I thought that the plan was that all of you were going to be married right here on this farm. Caleb, as glad as I was to hear you were coming home to visit and as hard as the boys and Nellie tried to get me not to chastise you, I need to let you both know how I feel."

Jennie, who had been listening rather tight-lipped, said, "Mrs. Carney, Caleb and I knew that if we were going to be together way up there in New York, we had two choices, getting married or living in sin. I know that the Sledge family doesn't rate very highly here in Sterling, but I and I'm sure my family are very happy we chose marriage and I was hoping the Carney family would be too."

Mother, who hadn't really known much about Jennie and probably only remembered her as that barn girl, who worked at Muldons, was visibly taken aback.

I started to say something but Mother said, "No, Caleb, let me apologize. Jennie, I'm truly sorry. I hadn't meant my anger about the situation to be a reflection of you. It's just that Hester and Emma's wedding here at the farm had been a salve for the wounds that Eunice's elopement had made. Then when my son does the same thing, runs off and gets married without any family invited or being involved, it caused a turmoil here. My criticism wasn't meant to reflect on you, so please forgive me. When the girls got married it was hard in some ways. But when Caleb, my little boy, went out into the world and married without me or any family it was a daunting hurt."

Jennie placed an arm on my mother's shoulder and said, "I can forgive you, Mrs. Carney. I can even understand your pain, but here's the thing. Look at Caleb; even I never want to forget the little boy Caleb, but the reality is that that is not the Caleb of today. The Caleb of today is a man, my man, and one who has promised himself to me, forsaking all others. This doesn't mean he no longer has a family. It only means that someone new is on the top of his pecking order. I am truly sorry that we couldn't have had a wedding here at the farm. Though Caleb mentioned it, there was no way under our circumstances we could figure out a way to do it without waiting another year and I'm sure you understand why we didn't want to do that."

"I know, Jennie, I know." Mother said. "Won't you please call me Mother, or Helena if you don't like using Mother? That Mrs. Carney bit from you makes me feel as if you think I might be to old to understand anything."

Jennie laughed and said, "That wasn't my thoughts at all, Mother. I just wanted it known that Caleb and I are not married because of some trap I set. We have known each other for a long time and it took all these years for us to realize this was meant to be and we both want everyone to be as happy about us as we are."

I wasn't sure after that exchange that Jennie would want to stay at Mother's house but Mother calmed down and became the caring mother I have always known.

"You two can take Emma's room," she said. "It's all cleaned and ready."

I looked askance toward Jennie.

She said, "You get our things, Caleb. I'll see if I can be of help in the kitchen. I can smell something delicious cooking there."

As surprised as I was at Mother's outburst, I was surprised more at the way Jennie handled it, going to the kitchen with Mother as if nothing had happened. Later with Jason, Francis, Nellie, Mother, Dad, Jennie, and I gathered at the table to enjoy one of Mother's roast pork dinners, I began to understand better about Mother's diatribe. It didn't really seem like home anymore with so much of the family gone. Mother apologized for the pork, complaining that it was hard to get decent pork now that we weren't raising our own.

Jennie laughed and said, "You would never guess there was anything wrong with it the way Caleb is wolfing it down. Now I know why Caleb always has that slight scowl when he eats my roast pork. Mother, you have to show me your secret before we leave. I wouldn't want to lose Caleb because I didn't know how to cook his favorite meal."

After we had eaten and Jennie and Nellie were cleaning up Mother asked, "Why don't you two run along now? I'm sure that Jennie is anxious to see her family."

Jennie looked more anguished then anxious but she dried her hands and we left.

When we were out of the yard she said, "I hope you don't think bad of me but let's not go to my house until tomorrow, in the morning probably would be better."

"I could never think bad of you, but your not wanting to go tonight is curious. Is there something wrong I should know about before we go to your house?" I asked.

"You can't be that dumb, Caleb. You have seen how badly my brothers have been beaten, and haven't you ever wondered why I always came running out whenever you came to pick me up?" she answered as she started to tear up.

"Oh, I had some ideas, but you and Janet seemed to not want to talk about your family so I never inquired. I know Janet left as soon as she could and that Arthur moved on shortly after I left town, but I haven't heard much about the rest of your family lately. Are things really that bad at your home?" I asked.

"Oh, Caleb! If you only knew how seriously I thought of asking you not to come back to Sterling for our first trip as a married couple. I couldn't make myself do that to you. You have a good family and I knew that Sterling and Mount Fay are deep in your heart and I would have to adapt to that. We can work that out, but when it comes to my family we have to do it my way. I'll go down by myself in the morning and lay some ground rules before we go as a couple. Is that going to upset you to much?" she asked, cuddling up closer.

"Upset me? Of course not. All you ever have to do is take the lead and I will follow when it comes to your family. After all, you didn't get a very warm welcome when we first met my mother either," I said with a laugh

The next day Jennie took the car, saying she had to pick up a few things at her house. When she came back a couple hours later I could see that she was upset. Mother asked if anything was wrong.

Jennie said. "It's nothing, Mother Carney. It's just that my sister had taken some things that were near and dear to me. I should have taken them before but I wanted to wait until I was in my own house."

Jennie and I spent time visiting friends and old haunts. Dad got us the address where Norman and Virginia were living now and we spent a day there with them. It was great to see them both again. Norman hadn't changed.

He kept saying, "I told you it should be Jennie all along, didn't I, Caleb, didn't I?"

Virginia asked about Joan and the other girls and we told her all we knew. She was happy that Betty and Etta had found someone and were married but seemed concerned when we told her about Joan's letter.

The last few days we were in Sterling we visited the boys at Muldons' farm, though there weren't many of the old crew left. The day before we left we spent the day wandering on Mount Fay. I thought that before we left, Jennie would want me to visit the rest of the Sledge family but it didn't happen so I let it be.

Soon we were on our way to Tupper Lake to spend a few days before we went back to work. We spent our days at the lake reliving our first dream date there, going out on the fishing boat during the day, enjoying the dinner cruise in the evening and making more passionate love at night. I think we both believed that no matter where life might take us we would have these times to hold on to.

Where life took us after our couple of days at the lake was back to Lawrenceville, Jennie back to the farm, and me back to the paper. After a couple of more years of reporting on late night meetings and an occasional fire or accident for excitement, it was clear that I wasn't making a big enough splash to give me a résumé that would advance my career.

I started putting more time into my freelance writing projects. Mostly all that was getting me was a bigger pile of rejection slips. Jennie and I started serious inquiries in any advertisement we saw that required a writer, and though there was some interest in me, there was nothing we thought was advancement from what I was doing.

I wrote some advertising jingles for a contest and was called in for an interview by some advertising outfit. There were no guarantees except a low paying three-month trial period and that meant moving to a big city. Though that looked like a fun job it was too much of a gamble and neither of us wanted to move to a city.

Eunice had written that Harry's business had expanded so much he was having a hard time keeping enough help in top management positions. I could well imagine that as Harry was hard on help, especially the first couple of hours of the day. I was glad for them, though it sure made my position in life look dreary.

A few weeks later I was finishing up a story of a couple who had just lost everything in their house to a fire. When I was interviewing them they told me about how all the mementos of their wonderful life together had been lost in the fire. Writing their story up got me to thinking about how, outside of Tupper Lake and our little heart pillow, little I had built of mementos in my life in the over five years we had been living here.

I was pretty much on a downer when I left the paper so I stopped in to the local pub to have a beer, hoping to develop a better mood before I faced Jennie. When I arrived home Jennie was just taking a pork roast out of the oven.

She shouted over the banging of the pots, "I'm glad you made it, Caleb. I think I finally made a roast pork that rivals your mother's. Tonight is a very special night for us."

Jennie was right. The pork was something to rival my mother's but for the life of me I couldn't think of anything about this date that was special.

Worried that I had forgot some important date of ours, I said, "I can't believe that I have forgotten an important date of ours. Please fill me in."

"It isn't something you forgot, but it's something I promise you that you will never forget. But no more questions until we have the supper dishes cleaned up," Jennie said with a little flirtatious laugh.

Her laugh eased my mind and after we had cleaned up and were sitting on the couch Jennie took both of my hands and said, "Are you ready for one of the biggest surprises of your life?"

The suspense and her coquettishness were exciting me, so I pulled her to me and with her head resting on my shoulder she whispered in my ear, "Caleb, you're going to be a father. I'm two months pregnant."

My world exploded. I had spent the afternoon worrying about not being anything and now I was going to be a father, but what kind of a father? I couldn't even satisfy my self so what would I have to offer a child? Jennie took my quietness for shock and she was right, but I couldn't let her know my true thoughts.

So I said, "Do you remember that first night at Tupper Lake when my tongue couldn't find the words? I feel the same beautiful intimidating wonder now that I felt then. I pray that this is an omen that your news tonight is going to turn out as wonderful as that night did for us."

The excitement of discovering you are to become a parent soon turns in to what is needed and how to get it. Jennie went on and on that night about all the wonderful things this meant. My mind couldn't wrestle past where my thoughts were that afternoon. I finally rested my mind and fell asleep by deciding first thing in the morning I would call Eunice and see if Harry has anything available that would support a family, because I sure didn't want the mother of my child to have to work.

Chapter 4

The day following Jennie's great announcement I called Eunice from the newspaper office and asked about the job openings that Harry had. My request made her suspicious but after getting her solemn promise that she wouldn't tell anyone, I told her about our situation. She was so excited, saying it's about time Hank got a cousin.

When she questioned me about leaving my writing position, I told her that I had given it my all up here for the last five years and I hadn't been able to make it a fulfilling or financially successful way of life. I told her that I intended to continue my freelancing but I needed a better income where I could provide for my family as a husband and a father. Eunice said she would talk it over with Harry and get back to me, but I asked her to wait for my call as I hadn't discussed this with Jennie yet and wanted to know what was available first.

I called Eunice a few days later and she said Harry would be very happy to have me back as he had many available positions. But what he needed most was an accountant that he would be comfortable with. He thought since I had a college education I could do that job and with a family member in that position, he wouldn't have the worries he has now about it. She also said that since the job paid much more than working on the buildings did, she thought the starting pay could be almost as much Jennie and I were making together now.

Though I had a college education, my mathematics and accounting studies had been the minimum I had been able to get by with, but I told Eunice I would brush up on it and make arrangements to move.

One of the men at work who had heard part of my conversation said, "I don't want you to think I'm nosy but I heard you talking about accounting. There's an advanced accounting class starting soon at the local high school three nights a week. It's something they do for the small towns around here to help keep local accounting departments up to par."

I thanked him thinking it might be smart to check the timing of it, if I was seriously thinking about doing Harry's accounting.

A few nights later Jennie said, "Caleb you look so worried lately. Aren't you glad we are becoming parents?"

"Of course I'm happy about it Jennie. In fact it was on my mind that we had better begin working harder at it before we got too old," I said with a laugh.

"I'll give you too old!" Jennie said slapping me side of the head. "Then why the hangdog look all the time lately?"

"You know Jennie our living like this has been heaven for me. What more could a man ask for than having a nice little home and a wonderful, understanding, caring, sexy wife to come home to every night. Still it's time we faced the truth, my writing just hasn't set the world on fire and the excitement of listening to a lot of blowhards at all these small town meetings has gotten to be a pretty boring way to make a living. I think that while I could hack this until we retired and found us a place to retire in Sterling, I think I owe a child a little better than just this subsistence life," I answered.

"Oh Caleb," Jennie said hugging me, "it won't always be like this. Someday what you write is going to be recognized and we'll be on High Street."

"I would like to keep on believing that Jennie, but I have been out of college for over six years and now I realize that successes are few and far between when writing usually by people who are already famous or write an occasional first novel that becomes a financial success. I don't want you to be angry, but I called Eunice and she said Harry has lots of opportunities for me," I answered seeing the fire rise in her eyes.

"I'm not going to get angry" she said, through clenched teeth, "but I do hope you're not planning on handing me some done deal and expect me to just go along."

"No, no Jennie, I wouldn't ever do that. I was just exploring available options. I plan to write to Jake and see if he knows of any opportunities in our field. He will have a better idea about what's out there from where he is in the city than I do from up here. I believe that both of us have known for quite a while without wanting to say it, that it is time for us to plan on moving on. Now that we are going to be parents, it's important that we get started. Don't you think doing some planning makes sense?" I asked watching her eyes slowly cool.

"I know Caleb, I know. It's just that these last five years have been so pleasant for me I didn't want to think of change. Go ahead, I'm ready now. I know you well enough to know there is more than you're telling me to your planning." she answered,

"Well one of the things Harry said was that if I could handle his accounting he would be able to pay me considerably more then we are both making here" I started as Jennie burst in.

"Caleb! I hope you haven't been talking to your sister about our finances! I would find that appalling," she shouted.

"No, Jennie," I answered, "I only said I was interested in finding a job that paid enough so you could stay at home and raise our children. That's when Harry mentioned what I could make as an accountant. But I'm not sure that I can handle Harry's accounting, his business has gotten big and it might need someone who understands the job more then I do. There's an advanced accounting class starting at night next week at the high school for town accountants and I am thinking of attending at least a couple of nights to see if it's something that would be of help. I'm not sure if accounting is what I want to do but at least it is another option we can plan with."

"Oh, Caleb!" Jennie exclaimed, "I wouldn't want to see you give up your dream of being a writer just because I'm pregnant."

"I'm not going to stop writing Jennie but maybe I can concentrate my efforts on a different kind writing if I'm not working for a paper. If I end up doing accounting, I would be at a desk all day and could write during any spare time I might have. As for writing being my dream, it was exciting in grammar school when Old Hanna singled Jake and me out. I will always be thankful for all she's done; first for her encouragement and then for the money she left us to further our education. Still, the truth is, I was lead into the field of writing, more then it being my dream. Oh, I would love to be a successful novelist but if journalism is just reporting the facts like I am now, I see it as more of a nightmare than a dream. I was told more than once in college that my writings were more story telling than journalistic. It may be that I would gain by getting out of the newspaper business."

"My hope, of course, is that I find my niche as a writer someday but I have already found a dream in my life with you. Now I have the prospect of having a houseful of little Carneys to share the dream with me." I answered, mentally thanking my father for insisting I develop a trade in addition to writing.

Jennie hugged me tight saying, "You're right Caleb, as long as we're together that's a dream enough for me, but for our children, we need to provide for more than just our contentment."

When I received Jake's letter he was all excited about me planning on coming back. Jake was assistant editor now and said he was sure he could find me a position at the paper. He not only had advanced at his job, he was married and they were expecting their second child any day.

I wasn't too interesting in going to another newspaper job but it did give us another option. So I wrote Jake, thanked him for his interest and told him I would keep him posted on my plans.

The only way I could attend the accounting classes was if I enrolled, the fees were minimal so I signed up. Mr. Ward, the instructor, was easy to follow and took us through the basics of accounting to see where he needed to begin the class. There were only about ten students and most of them were already working at some type of accounting. Most of them were keeping books for the small towns around Lawrenceville. With what I had learned in high school and college about accounting I was about as well prepared as the rest of the class.

After a couple of classes, I realized that my newspaper note taking lessons were very handy. Though I had to buy a couple of books that I couldn't find at the library to keep up, I found I was enjoying working with numbers more then I believed possible. As these classes were ending I spoke to Mr. Ward about why I took the classes. He suggested it would benefit me and my brother-in-law both if I took a two-month advanced class he was giving at the junior college starting in two weeks from now.

Talk at work about my attending the classes brought inquiries from my editor about why I was taking them. I was honest and told him that I was taking classes because I had been offered a well paying job in my brother-in-law's company as his accountant.

Jennie and I discussed the pros and cons of taking the two-month course at the junior college.

She said, "I think you should, but only if we are sure that taking that job is the right thing for us. I would be almost six full months along by the time you finish that course and I wouldn't want to be any further along then that when we move."

It wasn't that I was unconscious of Jennie's pregnancy but I hadn't given any thought of what the timing would mean, so I said. "I guess what we have to do is make a decision on whether working for Harry is the right move or not. I have a couple of weeks before I have to decide on the course. I have written Jake and asked if he could be more specific with job offers and expect to hear from him soon. I am more comfortable about Harry's job offer now than I was, but I don't want that to be the only option that we consider."

"I know Caleb, but it is unlikely that Jake is going to get you any position higher then being a reporter. Even if it pays well enough, are you going to be happy just continuing reporting for a newspaper? I have seen the interest you have taken in your accounting course. I believe you would be happier with your writing being your sideline rather then a deadline. I suggest that you have a serious discussion with Eunice about what the job entails. I f you require more schooling perhaps it could be done down there while you are on the job."

The following week while I was mulling over our situation at work and thinking how lucky I was to have such an understanding wife, the secretary came around with our pay envelopes. Stopping at the bank on the way hope I found my check contained a considerably higher amount then usual.

When I got home and showed Jennie, she said. "If this is going to be permanent Caleb, it's enough for us to survive here. That is another option that we hadn't considered."

The thought had crossed my mind when I first saw the check at the bank, but the truth was I was becoming bored and depressed with my job and had already discounted it, so I said, "It is exciting that they are attempting to keep me Jennie but we'll still only be surviving if we opt for that. I would be sorely tempted if it was only going to be the two of us but now that we are starting a family I want better then just survival."

"Here," Jennie said throwing me a couple of envelopes, "Maybe these will help, they came in the mail today. They're from Jake and Eunice. I waited for you to come home so we could open them together."

I opened Jake's first. After the basics he said that though he could probably get me top pay as a reporter, I probably had a long way to go before I could get a journalist position.

Next I opened Eunice's letter.

Dear Jennie and Caleb,

We are so excited that you are giving sincere consideration to coming to work for Harry's company. I'll try to make our situation more understandable to you. Harry was very lucky to get Shaq's uncle Edward to come to keep his books. The problem is, he only expected to get Harry setup and then turn the books over after a year so he could retire. Harry has hired two assistants to work with Edward and Edward has told him not to keep either one of them because they would steal him blind.

When Harry talked to Edward about you, he said if you had the rudiments of accounting he could teach you what you need to know in a couple of months. I also checked at the college and they have evening refresher classes all the time on almost every subject. Harry said he couldn't put a figure on a salary right away but if you can do as well as Edward, he promises you a very generous salary.

He said having Edward has shown him how valuable an

accountant can be because Edward has saved him thousands of dollars since he took over the books. I hope this all makes sense to you and that you do decide to take the job.

I don't know how much you have been keeping up with the Carney news but both Emma and Hester are expecting. It was quite a surprise for Hester as they told her that she couldn't have children but they both are very happy about it. Homer has finally found his niche in life; he has a job with Richard's company and gets to travel all over the country. Jason will graduate from college this year; Nellie has a steady who wants to put her on the stage as a mind reader. (I'm not sure what that's about, mother's words) Francis is now the head honcho at Muldon's barn (his words). Mother say's he often wonders what Homer and Caleb would think of that. Isn't the Carney news great? Mother's nest may be getting emptier but now she will have four grandchildren and Hank will have three cousins!

Hank still remembers you and can't wait until you return so he can wrestle with you. If I were you, I would eat my Wheaties because he isn't little Hank any more.

I'll close now with the hope to see you soon,
Your sister Eunice

Jennie was quiet for a while after I finished reading Eunice's letter. Then she said, "I guess that answers all our questions Caleb and it seems hands down that Harry is our best choice. I do wish they had been a little more open about the pay though."

"I'll call Eunice tomorrow to see if I can get a better answer on that Jennie, but I sense there is something else about this that is bothering you besides the money. Don't you think we should share our feelings on this?" I asked.

"Oh Caleb, it's just when I hear about your family and how close you all seem to be, I wonder if I'll be able to fit in. Living way up here I never have to think about being one of the girls from that Sledge family. I know it isn't like we will be living in Sterling but we can't avoid contact with Eunice and her family. I know you think I'm silly but think about it Caleb, not once have you ever been in my house in Sterling and I was only at yours once before

65

this last trip and that was because Etta was there. I'm sure your family feels as if they never got a chance to sift me for chafe and the very idea that you married a Sledge girl without that burns them," Jennie answered seriously.

"Let me tell you something, my mother never had a mean thought in her life and for years Homer has chastised me for the way I treated you by not knowing how you felt. I have always let your home life be your secret out of respect for you, thinking that you would share what you wanted with me. I never even questioned the fact that you didn't want me to visit there after we were married. I have no qualms about it at all, it's like if that's the way Jennie wants it, it's good enough for me. We have been married for over five years and held hands years before that, why all this now?" I inquired.

"Don't be upset Caleb, please. I don't know it must be those hormones they talk about. I just get to thinking there is going to be a new person on this earth and he is going to be a mixture of Carney and Sledge blood and I get anxious about what that could mean," Jennie said putting her arm around me.

"I'm not upset with you Jennie, I'm just nervous about all that is going on in our lives. Do men get hormone thingies too when their wives get pregnant? Tell you what, let's give all this talk a rest for tonight and try working off our hormone problems," I said with a laugh.

The next day at work the editor called me into his office and said, "Well how about it Carney, are we still going to lose you?"

"I can't give you a definite yet boss, but I will give you plenty of time to find someone replace me if Jennie and I make up our minds to leave. Thanks for the raise, it was a great confidence builder to feel you wanted me to stay that much."

"Since we got the journalism out of your writing you have become a very good reporter. We hate to lose that and know it will be hard to find someone else to cover all that copy for us. You do what's best for you and yours though and if you leave, please try to give us a month; now get out there and earn your raise," he answered

Later I got a call through to Eunice and asked if Harry could be more specific about the salary. She asked what I was getting now. I felt a little uneasy telling her because of what Jennie had said so I told her it varied and gave her the figure on my last pay check. She said she would get back to me as soon as she talked it over with Harry.

I had to cover a late meeting that night and when I got home Jennie said, "Harry called, what kind of a figure did you give him? He said he could start you off better than that and when you took over all of his accounting it would almost double."

I was stunned. It took me a minute to grasp what she had said. "Jennie, Jennie," I answered; "I gave them the figure on my last check saying my pay varied. If this means what it seems to mean, financially there is our answer. Now we have to decide how we feel about making this big of a change."

"Caleb, I am already carrying the big change in our life; and their offer means that we can own a house in a good neighborhood with good schools to raise our children. After you have mastered the job it will mean you may pursue any type of writing you want and when the day comes you are recognized maybe you'll be looking for your own accountant. Call Harry in the morning and tell them we need a month to say our goodbyes and clean up our obligations up here and then we will be down. Forget what I said about my fears of being a Carney and let's go to bed. I think we found the cure for my hormonal urges," she said, kissing me passionately.

The next day I called Eunice and told her what we had decided and that we would be in Oklahoma in about a month. At work I told the editor he had his month to replace me.

As I was leaving his office it seemed that every phone in the building was ringing. As the editor grabbed his phone he shouted, "Carney grab your gear and head over to Lacrosse and Allen Streets. There has been some kind of a big explosion."

I arrived there right behind the fire and police who were setting up a line to keep people away. Recognizing me as a reporter, one of the policemen let me inside.

There had been a terrific explosion, a propane truck that had just filled a tank at a triple-decker apartment building exploded as it pulled away. Part of the building was in shambles and it was burning furiously. The firemen had covered what was left of the truck with foam but it was too hot to approach. You could see part of the driver hanging from what was left of the cab it was evident that he was dead. I took pictures of the truck and then concentrated on the firemen fighting the fire in the building. They tried several times at different areas to enter the building but kept getting driven back, finally the chief called off all rescue efforts as some of the floors in the building started collapsing.

They had accounted for everyone except an elderly man and a teenage boy but it seemed impossible that anyone could still be alive in there. It took hours to bring the fire under control and it wasn't until the next day that the firemen, with the help of a wrecking crew's crane, were able to get the bodies out of the building.

I filed my first report using the picture of the truck and driver and pictures of the fire and firemen. The next day after congratulating me on my story the editor assigned me to follow up with stories from the police, firemen and any witness that might have been on the scene. He was especially interested in getting the story on the cause of the explosion.

It seemed strange the effect that having a by-line story like that made. The police, firemen and town officials now all seemed to know me and, except the few who found my truck picture too graphic, congratulated me on getting the facts straight.

Though I spent the next couple of weeks on the story and interviewed dozens of different people with many theories, there wasn't any concrete evidence as to what sparked the explosion. The only thing the gas company knew for sure was that at the time of the explosion the truck should have been almost empty. They hired an outside investigating group, who wasn't allowed to divulge any of their findings until cleared by the company. The state and federal governments had investigators sifting through all the evidence. All I could get out of any of the investigators was that it might be several months before they had an answer.

Knowing that I would not be here past the end of the month, my editor reassigned me saying, "Well, Carney, you may have come here quietly but you sure are leaving an image that will be remembered for some time around here."

It had been an exciting couple of weeks for me at work, which was going to make my leaving the paper a little harder than I expected. After work one night Jennie, who had been packing and helping to train her replacement at Jolene's farm, handed me a letter from Eunice saying, "What do you think of this Caleb?"

As I read the letter I began to understand the look of fire in Jennie's eyes.

Dear Jennie and Caleb,

I want you to understand there is no commitment on your part but a house a couple of streets over from us came up for sale and Harry was all fired up that we should put a retainer on it for you. Nothing would do but that I go with him and check it out. It is a real nice place! It has almost two acres of land, which is unusual around here. The house is about fifty years old but has been well kept up. It has a full cellar, three bedrooms, and a garage and is well landscaped. I know if I was you, having someone being that presumptuous would make me upset. Still, like I said, you are in no way committed to any deal but I couldn't stop Harry from putting a retainer on it. The house belonged to an older couple who has passed on and the estate wants to let most of the furniture go with the house. You don't have to be concerned about the money. Harry would only lose a small percentage of his retainer if you were not interested. After seeing the place, I would advice that you at least look at it and give it serious consideration. I only ask one favor, don't be angry with Harry. He sees this as a real good deal and wanted to save it until it you could at least have a look. He will understand if it turns out not to be what you have in mind.
From your busy body sister, Eunice

"This, my dear Caleb, is the kind of fear I tried to convey the other night. Presumptuous I'll say, the high and the mighty taking care of the poor little waifs. I lived under that cloud right up until the day I left Sterling and I'm not about to reenter a life that leaves me feeling that way again. You can call and tell Miss Queen Bee that her drone just lost his new accountant," Jennie said, shouting.

Knowing that now was no time to confront Jennie, I said, "I'll call first thing in the morning Jennie. It is a shame this had to happen but I truly understand how you feel. You should understand though that Harry and Eunice never meant to insult us. Harry's a go-getter, that's why his business is so successful. He just saw this as a good thing to do."

The next morning Jennie said, "Caleb please don't call Eunice today. Let's spend a couple days thinking about this. I'm afraid that part of what I feel is just another hormone driven emotion and I don't want our future hinged on that."

After a couple of days I called Eunice and told her we were not ready to own a house. We were thankful to Harry for thinking of us even if it seems like he put the cart before the horse. Eunice was gracious and only asked that we looked at the house to humor him.

The next couple of weeks were a whirlwind of packing and tying up loose ends. The crew at work had set up a little goodbye party at the local bar and we met there my last day after work. I joined in the fun and camaraderie for a couple of hours. As I started feeling the booze and remembered what happened to me when I drank beer with June; I begged off saying I had another commitment and a pregnant wife at home.

The Jolene's threw a big goodbye party at the farm and Mrs. Jolene said with tears in her eyes, "Jennie you have to promise you will stay in touch. It's like my daughter is leaving, not one of the help. Tomorrow I'm sending a man over from a moving company to figure out what you need for a truck to move your things; the help here decided that's what they want to give you as a going away present."

On the way home Jennie was as tearful as Mrs. Jolene had been, saying. "You know Caleb, leaving Sterling was like a escape but this is painful. I imagine it's like this in your family when someone leaves, huh Caleb?"

"Pretty much, Jennie, pretty much," I answered thinking, *looks like Sterling will always be a bone of contention between us. She feels she needed to escape from it, I dream of being able to return there.* "Homer always said it was like pages missing from a book every time one of us left. I built a kind of a wall in my mind to protect me from the pain of losing people after we lost Josh, but as it was, with the exception of Eunice, I was the next to leave. Though it saddened me to leave, I think my family was too excited about someone in the family going to college to be sad about it.

The moving man came the next day and as he was from the same company that we had been talking to, he said, "So you're the Jolene's princess that's leaving?"

"Now, don't make me any sadder then I already am. I hate to leave but life has a way of changing things," Jennie said patting her belly.

After checking out our things he left saying they would come to move us in two days.

We had decided that our car wasn't capable of such a long trip so we had already sold it and bought plane tickets to Oklahoma. We spent our last day and night reminiscing about our years there and how content we had grown.

Mrs. Jolene personally drove us to the nearest airport in Lawrenceville. Soon we were on a plane leaving the ground and I again felt like that little boy of years ago who was leaving Oscin on a train to face the unknown. Jennie wrapped her arms around me and suddenly I realized this was different, so much different.

Chapter 5

We landed at the airport outside of Lotus, Oklahoma shortly after noon and Eunice was waiting at the baggage pick up to meet us.

She gave Jennie a big hug saying, "You're pretty big, Jennie, how far along are you?"

"According to the doctor I'm only a little over four months, but I figure it's over five. Since I'm going to have to have a new doctor here we'll see what he says," Jennie answered, as she carefully checked Eunice out.

It dawned on me that since Eunice had left Sterling so long ago; they had never met.

So I said, laughing as Eunice hugged me, "I'm sorry, I don't believe that you two have ever been introduced."

Eunice said, "Oh hell, Caleb! Maybe we never met but she's family and family don't need that kind of formality. After all, it isn't like you're just coming home from your honeymoon with a surprise bride. She's been in the family for over five years and she's carrying a new Carney, the first one in a long time with that last name. I talked to mother the other night and she is really excited about the baby and real proud of you and Jennie."

Jennie laughed and said, "You know what, Eunice? If Caleb has his way and everything goes right on his new job, he's planning on trying to match your mother with Carney names."

Eunice took Jennie's suitcase and said, "You had better plan on having twins and triplets if you want to catch up with mother with your late start."

Listening to Eunice and Jennie talk as we walked to the car I felt better than ever about this move and it's effect on Jennie.

As we were driving back to Eunice's house, she said, "Jennie, I want you to be prepared for Harry and this house deal. I tried to tell him it was premature for you two to be dealing with buying a house right now, but as good of a man as Harry is—he is headstrong. It is probably one of his strengths though and why he has been so successful in his business. I'm telling you all this because I don't want you and Harry to get off on the wrong foot."

"Thank you for believing enough in me to be honest with me, Eunice." Jennie answered. "Don't worry though, I have some understanding of bullheaded men. Look at how long I had to wait to corral your brother."

"As long as you are allowing me to be honest Jennie, there is one other thing." Eunice said looking apprehensive. "Harry will be coming home early tonight and will want to rush you right over to see the house. He is still real excited about it, all I ask is you let him down easy."

"Look Eunice, we can do it his way as long as I get a chance to rest a bit before we go. Caleb and I can tell him that we need a couple of days to think on it, that way we can come up with some way to let him down easy," Jennie answered.

When we arrived at the house Eunice showed us to my old room which she had definitely feminized some.

Eunice said, "I hope you like the room Jennie. I want you to feel comfortable here so you won't feel that you have to rush into something you're not happy with while you two are looking for your own place. I have to go get Hank. He is at one of his friend's house and if I were you I would rest now because there won't be any resting for a while after Harry gets here."

After Eunice left Jennie said, "What's your take on Harry, Caleb? I never heard you talk about him like she does."

"He's a pusher, Jennie, but he isn't a monster. That is with the exception of the first couple of hours in the morning. He is just a go-getter. He will push his ideas to the limit but he certainly won't do it angrily, just strongly and Eunice is afraid it might cause problems between us. I believe if we stick to your plan everything will be all right. Now, you get some rest. I'll go downstairs and meet Hank when he comes in." I answered going out the door.

I'm not sure what I was expecting but it certainly wasn't this tall handsome broad shouldered teenage boy who came walking in with Eunice.

He walked over, put both hands on my shoulders, and said, "I hear you've been just waiting to get back so we could wrestle again, Uncle Caleb."

Not sure how he would respond, I gave him a little hug and said, "Right up until you walked through the door I thought I was young enough to wrestle you but seeing you like this—all grown up, I realized I might be too old and brittle boned to be wrestling."

He laughed saying, "It's great to have you back again Uncle Caleb. We used to have so much fun when you were here before. Maybe we can't wrestle but I have my own small Harley and if Dad will let me, I'll take you for a ride."

Eunice said, "I don't think that's going to happen for a while Hank. You haven't been riding yourself that long. I know that Dad has ridden behind you a few times but remember, he is an experienced rider and Uncle Caleb isn't."

Eunice, Hank and I spent the afternoon talking about the family and some of my escapades as a barn boy until Harry's truck came flying into the yard.

Harry came rushing in shouting, "Good to see you Caleb! Where is that beautiful wife of yours? Get her out here. I can't wait to show you the wonderful house I found for you."

Jennie, who by this time was already coming down the stairs said, "Well! So this is the wild man that you call your husband, Eunice? I thought I was being put on, but he does come on like a lion doesn't he? Well, here I am Harry! Caleb's beautiful wife, big belly and all."

Harry carefully gave Jennie a hug saying, "Eunice, you haven't been spreading stories about me again have you? Jennie, a woman is never more beautiful than when she's pregnant. Eunice and I wanted more children but it wasn't meant to be. However, the wise one gave us this strapping specimen you see over there with Caleb. Now that we are all acquainted let's go see the house."

Like Eunice had warned us, there was no stopping Harry. The house was only a couple of streets from Harry's so we decided to walk. We found the house about a hundred and fifty feet back from the road and we couldn't see it until we were almost in front of it.

What a house it was! It was a slightly oversized ranch with a garage connected by a breezeway. It had beautiful scalloped shaped foundation plantings with gardens along the driveway and a flowering hedge along the property line on both sides. It had a tremendous backyard with several trees that joined a wooded lot.

Inside there were three bedrooms, one and one half baths, a wonderful kitchen and living room and everything everywhere was immaculate. I heard Jennie a couple of times taking in her breath as if to keep from exclaiming.

Harry had been quiet all through our tour but after we came out he said, "What do you think? Isn't this a wonderful property? They are only asking twenty two thousand nine hundred and I think we can shave that a little."

"Harry, it is wonderful," Jennie said, "but you have to give Caleb and me a few days. This is to much too fast and we need time to digest some of what is happening to us before we even think of making this kind of a commitment."

"I only have a hold on it for two more weeks if that isn't time enough maybe I can get that extended." Harry answered pensively.

When Jennie and I finally got alone that evening she said, "God, Caleb, wouldn't that be a wonderful place to raise all those Carneys you're planning? I know it is one of those impossible dreams, a dream we can't afford to have, isn't it?"

"I don't know, and that's the problem. There are so many things to consider but we have two weeks so let's not stop dreaming yet. I was as taken by that property as Harry was, but I kind of tried not to let it get me. I tell you what I think, it's best we put off trying to make any decisions for at least a week, by then I'll have a better feel of what we can or cannot do." I answered, wishing I could have said we'll just buy it.

The next day I got to meet Edward the accountant. As he explained the books, he carefully questioned me in many different ways. I guess that was his way of testing me.

At the end of the day Harry popped in saying. "What do you think Edward, is he a keeper?"

Edward just kind of growled saying, "You can't know a book just reading the first chapter, ask me next week."

By the end of the week Edward had me doing most of the bookkeeping. His only admonishment was: if it wasn't clear then clear it in my head before I wrote it and if I couldn't, come to him. More than once I had to do that but he still seemed impressed with how I was learning his system.

Before we closed on Friday, he said, "Caleb, I don't want you to think I'm a busy body but Harry has talked to me about the house. I have a little understanding of real estate and I can tell you that you should grab it any way you can. Why, take those row houses over by Harry's house. Those houses sold from eight to twelve thousand when they were built, now ten, twelve years later they are selling for twelve to eighteen thousand and going up. The house you looked at with over a two-acre lot this close to a city like Lotus will be triple that price in ten, fifteen years. When you look at it that way, it is easy to justify buying it now, even if you only keep it for five years or so. If you can't swing it right now, I have advised Harry to buy it as a business venture. You can see by his books that it could be a good deal for him even as a rental property."

I thanked Edward and rushed home with my mind whirling with all that he said. Jennie and I had our savings but I didn't think we should use it as a down payment on a house. I told Jennie what Edward had said about the house.

She said, "Oh Caleb, does that mean we can buy it? It sounds like it is a win win situation as far as an investment goes."

"I'll talk with Harry about the banks around here and maybe Monday I can see if we would qualify for a loan that big. You know, Jennie, life is strange. When I was struggling with Josh's loss, it was Edgar who helped me see life straight. When I took Dad's place, it was Norman, Bruce and Virginia who were there to show me the way and now it's Edward and Harry. Besides that I am married to the girl who has been there for me forever, even when I was too dumb to know it."

Monday, I went to the bank Harry recommended and applied for a loan. The bank manager said he would put the application through but he doubted it would be approved because of my short employment record here.

When I went back to work I told Edward what had happened. He said, "That might be a problem ordinarily but I think the very value of the property will be to your advantage. Besides all of Harry's accounts are in that bank."

Jennie and I spent the next few days nervously waiting for their answer. Finally they notified us that they would approve the full amount minus Harry's retainer. Harry had put down twenty five hundred to hold it and though we could come up with that much it would all but wipe out our savings. After taking into account what Edward had said, we decided to take the plunge and buy the house.

Harry was elated. He said, "See, I told you!"

Eunice said, "It was to good of a deal not to hold it for them. This calls for a celebration. Harry's taking us all out for dinner."

At the restaurant Jennie said, "We really have to thank you Harry. All of us except you thought it was crazy for us to be thinking about buying a house right away. The house is like a dream come true. Like Edward says, even if it is a little over our heads, it is a very good time to buy a house because the market is going to keep going up. It will take Caleb and me a couple of days to get the twenty five hundred together for you Harry but we will have it by the end of the week."

"I want you to hold off on that. I have been talking to Edward about that and he thinks I can write it off as an employment cost, something about your moving expenses. So you just wait a while until he has that all figured out," Harry answered

The next couple of weeks were spent getting the house ready to move into. There was a stove, refrigerator and even a washer and dryer that went with the house and with what we had brought from New York, we had enough furniture to at least move in.

The first night we spent at our own home I found Jennie sitting on the bed with tears in her eyes.

Surprised I said, "Jennie all this rushing around hasn't been to much for you has it?"

"No, no Caleb. Before I came up I wandered around our property so elated and then it hit me. Here I am, one of the Sledge girls from Sterling who grew up in a shack, living in a dream house with the man of my dreams. I'm not sad, just emotional. I guess it's one of those hormone things again," she said, putting her head on my shoulder.

"I guess we know how to take care of that," I answered as we climbed into the bed.

By the end of three weeks, Edward decided he only needed to come in one day a week to check over the books. He would come and work with me when Harry started bidding on other jobs. The job became routine and I was able to spend more time with Jennie by the time our baby was born.

We had a baby girl and Jennie chose to name her Janet after her sister. Life was so great with my new job, our new house and Janet, I sometimes worried that it had come too easy.

About two years after Janet was born Jennie informed me there was another Carney on the way and soon Janet had a baby brother Josh. When Josh was about three years old I came home one night to find Jennie very ill. At the hospital they informed us that her illness was caused by a pregnancy and that there were complications.

They suggested that Jennie should stay in the hospital for a couple of days so they could run some tests. Eunice was with Janet and Josh and agreed to take care of them until Jennie was home and well.

The next day when I went to visit Jennie, she was crying and said, "I'm so sorry Caleb, we lost the baby."

I held her and tried to comfort by saying, "That's alright Jennie, we already have two and who knows maybe they'll be more."

Jennie just cried harder saying, "That's just it Caleb. The doctors say I need an operation and there won't be any more little Carneys."

"Well, I'll tell you what. It's okay, Jennie, we have already done our share. Anyway we can leave it up to my brothers to propagate the Carney name and if they are not up to it, there is always little Josh to help carry it on."

Jennie quieted saying, "Caleb, thank you. I thought you would be more upset after listening to you brag about beating your mother and father."

The doctors decided she should wait a few months to regain her strength before they operated. Jennie was despondent for a long time; we had been hoping things would be better after the operation. Still it was over a year after the operation before the Jennie I had grown to love and need so much, reappeared.

I don't know what I would have done if Eunice hadn't been there for the children and me. She worked magic at keeping the situation from harming the children. It was strange how Jennie came out of it.

One day while I was playing with the children, she said, "Caleb I think we should have a party to show Eunice how much we appreciate her caring ways."

Surprised, I asked, "What kind of a party do you have in mind Jennie, a cook out or a dinner party?"

"You know silly, a cook out in the back yard just like we always have," she answered laughing.

I hadn't heard her laugh for over a year and it was exhilarating to hear it again. We had her party and life regained its normalcy with Jennie almost like nothing had ever happened. I discussed this with Eunice and the doctors and everyone advised me it was probably better not to dwell on it or mention it to Jennie.

About a year after Jennie's illness we received an alarming letter from mother.

Dear Caleb and Jennie,

As you know from your last trip home, your father was being forced to retire because of his age. He couldn't admit to himself that he could no longer cut the mustard, as he puts it. The new logging equipment and mills are much more demanding in skills than your father possesses. Even though he could have retired a few years ago, he fought for jobs and for a while he was successful. Finally he was told he was just to old and he couldn't find a job. I have kept this from you before because I didn't see the need to burden you with problems. Now I am at my wits end, it's been over a year since he has had a job and he has become withdrawn. As you know there is little left to do here on the farm, the horses and the cow are gone and we stopped raising pigs long ago. We do still keep a few chickens and I often wonder if we had kept some of the animals if it wouldn't have been better for him. Money is not a problem, we have enough coming in to keep us going but I am very worried about your father. He sometimes doesn't speak for days. I am sending a similar letter to all your brothers and sisters with two things in mind. First, that you all will be aware about your father and second, maybe one of you will have an idea that will help.

Love to You, Jennie, Janet and Josh
Mother & Grandmother Carney

Jennie, Eunice, Harry and I discussed what, if anything we could do about Dad every time we were together.

One time when we were discussing Dad, Harry said, "I've been thinking. You know when something goes wrong with a family member in the tribes; they all work together with whoever is in trouble to find a solution. Would it be possible for as many of your family to get together at your Dad's farm to help your mother with this? I'm not sure if that's the answer or not but I think it's worth a try."

Eunice and Jennie thought it was a terrific idea and starting making calls and writing letters to set a date. It was only two months later that we were on a plane flying back. Taking a plane made it possible for Harry to go because he couldn't be away so long. The last time we drove but Harry couldn't come and the long drive wasn't very pleasant for the children.

We couldn't get a flight into the airport by Oscin so we arranged for Aaron and Emma to pick us up in Connecticut. Because there were seven of us, Aaron brought one of his company's vans.

When we got to the farm we were quite a crew: Harry, Eunice, Hank, Hester, Richard, Ricky, Aaron, Emma, Lena, Laura, Jennie, Janet, Josh, Jason, and me. Homer was clear across the country and couldn't get back, Nellie was over seas doing research and Francis had just taken a job managing a big farm upstate New York and didn't think he should leave.

Mother was sad all her children couldn't come but was ecstatic at having all her grandchildren there. I think we kind of scared Dad because he disappeared into the barn shortly after we arrived. After we had all gotten settled I went out to find Dad. He was out in the wood lot sitting on a stump. He looked so old and lost that I decided not to speak at first; I just sat on a log close by and waited for him.

Finally he said, "Caleb, it's good you all came. Mother needs to see more of the family, it's hard on her with most of you being so far away and being so busy with your own lives. I don't think she ever imagined it would be like this when we grew old."

I didn't know quite how to answer that as I set looking at how much my dad had aged because what he said left me feeling a little guilty. I tried saying, "Dad I have to tell you the truth one of the reasons we are all here is that mother has become worried about you lately."

"It seems so wrong, Caleb, to grow old like this. You know, when I was laid up after my accident, as bad as it was there was always some hope, but there is no cure for old age and it stinks. Since I no longer can hold a job I feel like I am not a whole man and everyday there is a new ache or pain and now my water works aren't functioning very well."

I had several quick thoughts that I might have answered him with but decided that it would be better if I waited until I had a chance to discuss some of this with the others.

So instead I said, "We all will grow old, Dad, but if we are lucky we will all have a life to look back on that is as good and honest as yours is."

"Maybe that's my trouble Caleb, looking back isn't my thing. I always was looking ahead hoping to make things better, trying to gain ground not lose it. Now what's ahead isn't gaining, though not especially fearful it sure isn't ground gaining." Dad answered.

Not sure how to answer that I said, "Well, are you up to going back and facing your big family? I'm sure you don't want your grandchildren growing up thinking their grandfather is afraid of them."

Dad and I went back to the house and as all the grandchildren gathered around us, I could see a semblance of joy on his face.

Our visit was only going to be a couple of days so after we had eaten, I said, "I, for one, want to take a walk around the farm and since we aren't likely to all be here together again, how about all my brothers and sisters joining me?"

"Well!" Richard said, "Does that include brother-in-laws, too? I could use a work out to walk off your mothers cooking."

Laughing, Mother said, "This is just like the old days! Everybody sneaking off and leaving me to clean up and do the dishes."

Hank, guessing what I was up to, said, "Not everybody, Grandma, all of us grandchildren will stay and help."

Mother was real pleased with Hank's idea so we left and spent an hour walking and discussing Dad's situation. Though it seemed rather weak, the best we could come up with was we needed to get him in for a complete physical exam. Knowing that he probably would rebuff Mother if she tried to force him alone, it was decided that we should do it as a group.

Later that evening when Dad joined us, we discussed it with him. At first he was a little angry saying, "Is this why you're all here?

To ship me off to some doctor's office?"

"No, Dad," Eunice answered, "that isn't it at all! We have been trying forever to get as many of us here at one time and this time we were able to get most of us here. While we were walking Caleb told us how you seemed to be having painful days and though there isn't a cure for every thing, there is medication to make pain easier to live with."

To my surprise, Jennie spoke up and said, "Dad Carney, besides wanting to get together, we wanted our children to see their wonderful grandparents and cousins as often as we can. Our concerned is because we are hearing that one of these grandparents is suffering needlessly."

Janet who had been taking this all in, walked over to Dad and said, "Mommy makes me go to the doctors too. I never want to go but the doctor makes my hurt go away. Now grandpa, you should go and let him fix your hurt."

We were all a little taken back by Janet talking to Dad like that. Dad said, "Hearing it like that from such a voice of authority, Janet, I guess I have no choice except to have you grandmother make me an appointment."

We all laughed when Janet said, "You have to cross your heart and promise, Grandpa."

Dad laughed with us as he drew an X across his heart saying, "You mean like that, Janet?"

Before we all had to go, Mother had made an appointment for Dad and promised to let us all know how he made out.

On our last day, Mother asked, "Did you put Janet up to talking like that to your father?"

"No, Mother, it just came out of the blue but I have noticed that Janet seems to have that same sixth sense that Nellie always had. I'm not sure if that's a good thing or not. I know Nellie used her gift carefully but it must have been scary for her sometimes," I answered.

I wanted to climb Mount Fay before we left but knowing it had never been a part of Jennie's and my past, I was hesitant to broach the subject.

Luckily, Janet asked, "Aren't we going to climb your mountain before we go back?"

Jennie said, "That's a good idea, Caleb. Why don't you take the children for a hike up the mountain? It will be good for them just before we leave for the plane."

When we got to the mountain. Janet was all for climbing all the way to the tower but I figured that would be too much for Josh who wasn't quite five yet so we went to the ledges and I showed them the cave Karl and I hid in when we were kids.

Janet was all excited and said, "Tell us again about that bad kid, Bob who was always chasing you two."

I retold the story, of course I left out the reason he was chasing us. It was good to be back on the mountain with my flood of memories and watching my own children exploring. I knew standing there then on the mountain with my children and all my memories that someday, somehow I was meant to come back here. These emotions again brought to mind Josh's mountain poem, so I recited the first verse.

I know she's not very big as mountains go, but she has a grip on my heart, in a special way

That mountain that hovers above my hometown, so aptly named Mount Fay

Her name in legend is for a little girl who died there in her mother's arms

While a captive of some Indians returning from a raid on the farms

There are those who say it isn't true, this legend of how her name came to be

But no matter how others have named her, Mount Fay is my mountain to me

"Is Uncle Josh's poem why you call this your mountain, Dad?" Josh asked.

"That's a big part of the reason, Josh," I answered as we reached the trail back down.

The children wanted us to race down, like in my stories. Running down the mountain with my children, the wild beating of my heart seemed to say, it has to be, it has to be.

Riding back to the airport with Richard and our group, I started having that old feeling of being torn away from Sterling and Mount Fay again, maybe forever. Jennie, sensing my mood reached over and held my hand.

It was about two weeks after we arrived back in Lynbrook that we received word about Dad. They had put him on medication for his arthritis and also an anti depressant, though they didn't tell him. This was very helpful but the bad news was that his problem of his water works, as he called it, was an enlarged prostate and they wanted more tests before they try any treatment.

A week after we received that news, Mother called all upset. Dad's problem was cancer and it was not just in the prostrate, the cancer had invaded other parts of his body. The doctors hadn't finished their evaluation yet but had already hinted that it might have gone so far that there might not be much they could do for him.

I didn't think when we saw Dad last that any of was prepared for anything as devastating as this. It had been shock enough to have to start thinking of him as being old. I knew Dad was well into his seventies but until our last trip, despite his bad limp I hadn't thought of him as old.

Harry suggested that Eunice should plan to fly down to be with mother until we found out what is going to happen. He suggested that she could take turns with the other children if things got bad.

Within the week, Mother called very, very disturbed. The doctors had decided that to operate not only would be useless; he probably wouldn't live through the operation.

Eunice, who had taken Mother's call, immediately packed and arranged for a flight home.

As we drove her to the airport, Jennie said, "Eunice, if you decide the children wouldn't be too much for your parents, then there isn't any reason why we can't go down and spend a week or so before school starts."

"Thank you, Jennie, you really have become a true Carney, haven't you? I will let you know as soon as I can find out what the rest of the family's plans are," Eunice answered just as we arrived at the airport.

A little over a week after Eunice left, she called the house saying, "Caleb, you had better come down. It's real bad, Dad's system is starting to shut down and the doctors say it is only a matter of a week or so."

I couldn't get a flight in that direction until two days later and when Homer picked me up at the airport, he said, "He's gone, Caleb. Dad's gone. God, this is hard to take. What are we going to do without him here?"

Homer's greeting left me so emotional that I couldn't answer so I just held him with tears streaming down my face.

Later riding in the car after I had regained my composure, I asked, "Has anything been done about burial arrangements?"

"You know, Caleb, I never heard about it, but it seems Mother and Dad had made all their arrangements way back when Dad had that bad accident. I am happy that they did, because it will be the way they want it, not left to us to decide for them. Mother has decided to have the services and burial next week, hoping to give all the family time to get here," Homer answered.

When we arrived home, I was surprised how well Mother seemed to be taking things.

I held her for a few minutes saying, "I feel so bad, Mother. If I could have gotten a plane sooner, I might have made it in time."

Mother said, "He wouldn't have known you, Caleb. He wasn't conscious the last few days and timing in situations like these are in God's hands, not ours. He knew he was going and the last day we talked he said to tell the children not to be sad and that he loved them all. I want them to look at my services as a time for family to be together like we all will be again someday."

After hearing all this, I needed to be alone so I went for a walk out to the woodlot where we used to cut our wood. Sitting on the same stump where Dad had sat when we had talked here last time, I wondered about his words. Father certainly hadn't been an ardent churchgoer and his last words kind of surprised me. I knew that was the position of our church and though I wanted to be a believer, sometimes I found myself wondering. I sat for some time pondering life and its ending and decided that Dad must have seen a truth like we all will probably see at end of our time here on earth.

When I got back to the house, our pastor was there discussing what Mother wanted at Dad's services. Mother handed him a copy of what had been decided. After looking it over, the pastor asked if there were any special stories or traits that she wanted mentioned. Mother told him she wanted to put that off until the whole family could contribute and she would call him when that happened.

Two days before the funeral, all the family had arrived, even Nellie who had managed to get a flight back from Africa. The place was chaos with people trying to find places to sleep and with all of the grandchildren running around. I thought Dad would really smile to see all of this.

At the service, Eunice gave the eulogy. They had asked me as the oldest son but I knew I wouldn't be able to hold it together. The church was full with people, some even having to stand in the next room.

At the graveyard in the shadow of the mountain as we were all saying our last goodbyes to Dad, I thought about the last of Josh's mountain poem, which was etched in the back of his gravestone.

Born I was beneath her slopes, with her woods echoing back my lives searching cry

And my grave will lie within her view when I say my last goodbye

Chapter 6

Life was surreal for months after losing Dad. Harry had about ten different jobs going so I had to put more hours than usual at work; I found being busy was a blessing. Eunice, I, and the rest of the family had great concerns for Mother now that she was alone at the farm. She insisted that she wasn't going to leave her home despite offers from the family who had homes to have her come live with any of us.

For the next few years even though some of us had to travel a long way, we took turns in making sure one of our families would be there for visits every couple of months. Jennie, Janet and Josh would go down for a stay when the children weren't in school. I would fly down for at least one long weekend while they were there.

Mother had always enjoyed good health and seemed content with her life and she enjoyed having the children come. It seemed strange now when I visited; no cow, pigs or horses though mother still kept a few chickens. I had dreamed of teaching little Josh how to milk, so I missed having a cow there. I took him to Muldons one night at milking time, but everything there was different now. Strippers were no longer needed and they had actually added a small milk parlor like the one at Jolene's farm where Jennie had worked.

I didn't know any of the men doing the milking but they were good to Josh and showed him how to squirt milk from the cow's teats. He got really excited about it and they even let him try himself. On our way home I told him all about how his mother and I had worked there when we were young and how different it was now.

When he got home he ran to Jennie saying, "Mom! I got milk out of a cow just like you and daddy used to do."

Jennie laughed and said, "That's good Josh, now when Daddy starts telling those wild stories about his barn boy days you'll know where he is talking about. How was your trip back to the barn, Caleb?"

"You know, Jennie, life really does go on, even in our old haunts. You wouldn't recognize the old barn, everything has been remodeled and they have added more space, a milk parlor, and even an automated milk room. No more strippers or crazy parties out by the watering trough. I guess that puts meaning in the old saying, you can't go back," I answered wistfully.

"Why, Caleb Carney, don't tell me that you're pining for the old days, as good as we have it now, are you?" Jennie asked with a quizzical look on her face.

"I don't know about pining, Jennie, but seeing those changes I felt like I used to when I would lose something important to me when I was a kid. I think that maybe you would have felt some of that nostalgia too, if you had been with us. Remember it was those times that brought us together," I answered.

Jennie hugged me saying, "For that I shall be forever thankful Caleb, but the truth is, during my last years on that job and living in Sterling, I felt trapped and with the exception of missing you, I was glad to be leaving."

Knowing how different Jennie and I were about Sterling and our lives here I didn't push it. Still it always amazed me that despite how close we have become there was still some of Jennie's life that I was not a part of, and probably never would be.

Janet came running in and said, "Daddy you took Josh to the barn without me. I think it's only fair that tomorrow you take me up to the tower. Last time we couldn't go way up because Josh was too little and I want to go to the top of your mountain."

Jennie laughed and said, "See where the wild stories of your Sterling youth gets you? I'll give you this though, you do make your youthful episodes sound exciting."

I patted Janet's head and said, "I think that's a great idea. Maybe it would be best if the whole family went. Josh is old enough now, how about it, Jennie?"

"I really can't Caleb, your mother and I have plans for tomorrow but since it's your last day here I think you should take the kids," Jennie answered walking away.

The next morning the three of us drove to the foot of Mount Fay and started our climb. Josh who was over six now wasn't having any trouble; in fact I was the one who needed to stop to rest.

About halfway up there was a vaguely familiar figure sitting on a log. As we drew nearer I knew I should know him but I wasn't sure.

He had a half smile on his face as he said, "If it isn't my brother-in-law Caleb! What brings you back to the mountain?"

At first the brother-in-law business set me back then I recognized him. It was Jennie's brother Arnold, so I said, "Long time no see, Arnie! Have you shot any wild cats lately?"

Arnie laughed saying, "Man, that was a long ways back, wasn't it, Caleb? I wish life was that simple now, How's my uppity sister? You know she disowned the family after moving to New York, only visited once and even then she didn't stay long. We knew you two had married and were in town several times. Mother was distraught for days when she didn't visit. I suppose these little waifs are your children. Is it allowed that I can be introduced as their uncle?"

Not knowing the why of Jennie's actions, I couldn't in all good conscience refuse, so I introduced him as Uncle Arnold, Mom's brother.

Janet was excited to learn that her mother had a family and started asking Arnie all kinds of questions. Where his mother and father lived; did he have any brothers or sisters. Arnie looked at me as if for permission, I shrugged my shoulders not knowing what to say.

"Well little Janet," Arnie started, "I have a sister named Janet and it wouldn't surprise me to know that is where you got your name, just like your brother here got his name from your daddy's brother Josh. I had a brother named Arthur, who was killed in the Korean War. Your daddy knew him well. Both of them worked at Muldons when they were kids, along with your mother and aunt Janet. My mother and father still live in Sterling, if you can call living what they do. Janet doesn't get home often but she does visit once in a while. My sister's were my protectors and after they both left, I joined the Army but was discharged with a medical two years later. I didn't move back home but I do visit both my folks and this mountain. I come to this mountain because it holds some of the best memories of my youth."

Josh was getting anxious saying; "Come on, Daddy. Let's go find the tower."

Janet, who had inherited some of the sixth sense that my sister Nellie had, was so enthralled with what Arnie was saying that she didn't want to leave.

Arnie settled that by saying, "I wish we could talk more, little lady Janet, but Josh has to find his tower and I have an appointment that I better be getting to."

Janet had a million questions that I couldn't or didn't dare answer. My mind was full, after the little peek that Arnie's talk had given me of life at the Sledge house. Recalling the times Arthur had came to work looking like he had lost a boxing match, made a disturbing image in my mind.

Soon, though, Janet and Josh's excitement as we neared the tower erased my thoughts as I began remembering the full glory I felt my first time of reaching the tower. Though we couldn't get in to the little room at the top, Josh insisted on climbing all the way up. Janet stopped about half way and went back down. As much as I understood Josh's excitement and desire to go all the way up, the truth was now I found myself feeling queasier then I ever had felt before. After we came back down, we sat at the foot of the tower and ate the snack Jennie had prepared for us.

While we were sitting there Janet said, "Daddy, tell us about Uncle Josh and his mountain poems."

We talked about Josh and how he had loved this mountain and how many of the poems he wrote had to do with his experiences here. While I was searching my head for an appropriate poem for this trip up the mountain his Woodland Place poem came to mind. Hoping I would get it right I recited:

Father took me by the hand and led me to the wood

And spoke to me about the trees until I understood
Some had grown for us to use, for house and for chair
Then he taught me to tell apart the different species there

Then he took me to a place that I was sure would be
The prettiest scene in all my life, I would ever see
A stand of tree so straight and tall they seemed to reach the sky
And every kind that he had taught, were mirrored in my eye

So enchanted was I then, with the woodland place
I made this vow so loud and clear; it brought a smile to fathers face
Never shall the woods mans axe be laid upon these trees
Never shall the paths of man destroy their majesty
Your beauty shall lay untouched let others come and see
And wait the day that I return and bring my child with me

After reciting, I thought how beautifully Josh's poetry described life. I was feeling suddenly sad that it was me, not him, bringing children to his mountain.

Young Josh, evidently remembering some of my mountain stories said, "Come on Dad, let's race to the bottom like you used to."

I soon found I wasn't the young boy who used to do this and half way down convinced Josh we should rest a while.

Janet started right in with twenty questions about Arnie. "How come Mommy hasn't told us about him? Why haven't Josh and I ever met our other grandparents? Why did Uncle Arnie seem so sad? What did he mean Mommy and Aunt Janet had protected him?"

I stopped her by saying, "It's time to get going Janet and you'll have to wait until your mother decides to answer all those questions because I will probably answer them all wrong."

As we raced the rest of the way down, I toyed with the idea of telling the children not to mention Arnie to their mother but decided that wouldn't be right.

As we were getting into the car Janet said, "Uncle Arnie is a very troubled man, isn't he, Daddy? I could just feel it as he was talking. I'm not sure what was bothering him but it was big."

I didn't answer, but her Nellyism sixth sense was becoming more noticeable every year and I had prayed she would be able to handle it as well as Nellie had.

At home Janet ran into the house before Josh and I had hardly gotten out of the car. By the time we came in Jennie was already afire, and if looks could kill, I would have dropped dead right there.

I said, "What could I do, Jennie? He was just there sitting on a log beside the trail and wanted to talk to the children."

Jennie just glared at me saying, "Come on, Josh, I want to have a private discussion with the both of you."

As they left the room, Mother came in saying, "What's the problem Caleb? I don't believe I ever have seen Jennie look that mad."

After I explained, Mother said, "I have often wondered why we never met any of her family, not even after you were married, but I figured there were some problems that you and Jennie wanted to keep to yourselves, so I never interfered. I can't believe having her children meet her brother would make her so upset though."

I wished that I could be there with them as Jennie tried to answer all of Janet's questions. I knew that Jennie would get herself under control and do the right thing by the children but I couldn't help but wonder what that could be.

I had to leave early the next morning so that night I said my goodbyes the children and tucked them in when they went to bed.

As I was leaving Janet's room, she said, "Daddy, Mommy said that the next time we came to Sterling maybe we could meet her father and mother."

When Jennie and I were alone, Jennie said, "I'm sorry Caleb, after I talked to the kids I realized you were very careful in anything you said and you couldn't help running into Arnie. I probably have handled this all wrong. My first visit here after I went to New York I decided I would no longer be a Sledge girl and forget all about my family. It has worked for me for years but now I realize that what a conundrum I have created for my children. I'm not sure there is any good answer but we are only going to be here for another two weeks so I have decided to try and come up with a good answer by the time we come back again. Arnie is not a bad man; Janet told me that he has some mental problems probably from all the beatings he took as a kid. After

Arthur was killed he was really bad for a while, that's why he was discharged from the Army. Janet used to keep me informed about the family but in the end I tried burning her letters without reading them so I could forget, yet sometimes I opened them. The last time I corresponded with her was a few years after we were married though she kept writing every couple of months. You know Caleb, I have had some good talks with your mother about a lot of things and I wondered what you thought about me confiding in her before I leave?"

"I'm glad you brought that up Jennie. I was just thinking that might be a good idea myself. Mother has a lifetime of experience to lean on and she would never be pushy about what she thought and would be more than willing to share any ideas she thought would be helpful.

When I got back to Lynbrook, Harry had two more jobs that he wanted to bid on so I was busy for the next couple of weeks figuring material and labor cost. Harry was very good at figuring the labor hours and would give me his estimates to price, and then we would add a booked percentage. Harry business was so big now, he had a couple of other men who did the preliminary work on needed materials, so though it wasn't a complicated process it sometimes was a long one.

Jennie and the children were back and Janet was still buzzing about her Uncle Arnie.

When I asked how that was going Jennie said her discussions with Mother about her family went very well and Mother had some good ideas.

"Your mother wanted to go visit my folks after I left, thinking she would be more help to me after meeting them. At first I was horrified but the more your mother talked about it the more it seemed to make sense. So we decided that she should; now that I'm back here I'm not so sure about it."

I held Jennie and said, "One thing you don't have to worry about, Jennie, is my mother making things any worse, and I believe this could be a big help for you."

A few months after Jennie came back, Willy who now was one of Harry's foremen came into my office and said, "What the hell is going on with Harry? Half of the men are ready to quit. Everybody was used to his surly moods in the morning but now no one can do anything right, anytime of day."

"Harry doesn't spend much time with me once the bids are out so I haven't seen much of him lately," I answered, "How long has this been going on, Willy?"

"It's been over a week and most of our new guys are ready to quit. He's going to be in a hell of a mess if that happens. He's short of help now and he just started two new jobs. I tried to talk to him about this but he just blows me off. I'd quit myself if I weren't so old and can't climb anymore. Somebody has to do something, Caleb, or the whole company might collapse." Willy said, as he walked out of the room looking like he was ready to cry.

I called Eunice and asked what was going on with Harry, she said, "Come over as soon as you can, Caleb, and we'll talk."

Eunice sounded really sad so I closed the office early and rushed over.

She said, "Caleb you have to help. Harry won't even talk to me; he leaves early in the morning and comes home late. You know Hank wanted to join the R.O.T.C. while he was in college. He was always very interested in the military but Harry always put it down and they often argued about it. After college Hank did what his father wanted and came back to join him in the business. Even though he had worked summers with his dad, Harry insisted that he should start at the bottom and learn the business from the ground up. I have never said anything but I knew things weren't working out for Hank and he wasn't interested in taking over the business some day."

"About a week ago, right after Harry started those last two jobs, while he was on one of his morning tirades Hank challenged him and told him it was stupid to act like that. Harry started climbing all over him, Hank calmly packed up his tools left the job and went to a recruiting station and joined the army. When Harry found out what he had done, he threw all of his things out of the house and it's been hell here every since. I have kept it quiet because I thought I could calm him down, but I have failed," Eunice finished, by now in tears.

Having worked for Harry, his moods weren't new to me, but damned if I had an answer to this, so I said, "I'm so sorry Eunice, I don't have an answer right off the top of my head but let me think on it and try to plan something. The last thing we need is to have Harry's temper ruin everything he has built over the years."

When I got home I confided in Jennie hoping talking would help produce a glimmer of an idea.

Jennie, who knew me better than I knew myself, said, "Caleb, this is going to take more then just you. In his anger Harry will just see it as Eunice's brother sticking his nose in. Do you know any of his men besides Willy that might be of help? I think this has to be approached as a job thing, rather then from the family side. If he can be made to see what is happening to his business because of his behavior, maybe that will help the whole situation."

Most of the men outside of Willy were new to me since I didn't go onto the jobs but Kale who was retired, now stopped into the office once in a while. I thought of Shaq, he ran his own small business now but Harry used him whenever he had too much welding to handle with his own crews. After discussing this with Eunice I contacted Shaq, Willy and Kale and it was decided that the best thing to do was to pick certain men from each of the crews and have a intervention with Harry about the effect his anger was having on his business.

Willy, Kale and Shaq called the men they picked over the weekend and asked me to arrange to have Harry at my office first thing Monday morning.

When I opened my office Monday there were already about twenty-five men there and Kale said, "There's more to come Caleb, I called some of the old guys too."

Harry came roaring in on his old Indian shouting, "What the hell is going on here, Caleb? Why the hell aren't these men at their jobs?"

I knew there wouldn't be room enough in my office so I brought out a chair and asked Harry to please sit down.

"Now Harry, these men have come to me with a problem, I know it isn't my place to deal with the men but they were stuck, I told them that you were the only one who could solve their problem so they asked me to arrange this meeting. I told them that you would hear them out, so if you have any respect for me, please at least do that."

Though I managed to get that all out I was really out of my element as far as leading anything like this and was really pretty scared of what might happen.

Harry glared at me for a minute and then sat down and said, "Spit it out, I can't have my men wasting time because of somebody's damn foolishness."

Willy went first saying, "Harry, you know I am one of the few men left from your original crew. With that tight crew, your hell on wheels act every morning was acceptable and as your crews grew we had been able to convince them to accept it. Now, you have crews in the hundreds, most who you hardly know you or you them. Lately with your all day, everyday haranguing, you are about to lose so many good men that you won't be able to keep your jobs going."

Harry started to get up but Shaq jumped in with, "Hold on Harry, it's a lot more than just losing good men. These men have worked hard for you and count on their paychecks and it doesn't seem fair that they are being punished because you are so upset about something. If you don't care about them, think what this could mean to all that you have built over the years. Losing men and getting behind on jobs will start rumors like Jackstone's Steel is starting to collapse. Now no matter what your heartache is now, think of what that would feel like."

Kale jumped in saying, "Harry, I'm an old man and among my regrets is how much of my life I wasted in anger about something that could have been cleared up with an honest approach and a little talk with those involved. I, for one, have always been proud I was a part of Jackstone Steel and would hate to see it go down the drain because you can't control your temper."

It was quiet for a moment and Harry said, "Is that it?"

One of the younger workers spoke up, "One of the proudest moments of my life was when you gave me a raise and said I had proved you right in hiring me. Still I have to agree, no one should have to take the abuse you been handing out just to keep a job. One other thing, if your foremen haven't told you, I will. All of your jobs are falling behind because of the way you been acting."

Harry stood up and said, "I don't know whether to thank you or kick your butts, but I have listened and I promise to give every word deep consideration. Now go back and get those buildings raised."

After they all left Harry came into the office and said, "Thank you Caleb, I have been in such a rage about Hank, that I haven't been able to think or see straight. God, it's hard to believe I have even jeopardized my company. I'm going around to each job and turn them over to my foremen for a few days."

I said "I think that is a good idea Harry and you should talk this out with Eunice, too."

That night I got a call from Eunice.

She said, "I don't know what you did Caleb, but when Harry came home he apologized and told me that he was taking a couple of weeks off and we should go on a trip anywhere I wanted to go. I asked if it would be all right if we went to Sterling and spent some time with Mother. He said that was a good idea and maybe he should spend some time on that mountain Caleb is always talking about. I'm not sure that he can stay away that long without getting antsy about his business but I sure hope so. He said Shaq was going to fill in for him while we are gone since you and he have proved you two could handle anything."

I knew that Shaq had enough experience about any one job to be okay but I wondered about him having so many jobs to watch. Shaq asked Kale to come and help. With him and Willy and a couple of the other foremen, in a week all the jobs were back on schedule. I figured Harry would be calling twice a day but he didn't. I found out later that a couple of days before they left, Harry had gone to talk to someone and had been advised he needed to get away from everything or he was headed for a complete breakdown.

Two weeks after they left Eunice called and said, "Caleb, please tell me that everything is going all right."

"It is, Eunice, much better then I expected. Shag and Willy have all the jobs on schedule or better. You tell Harry he did a good job of training Shaq and his foremen and that Kale is inspecting welds on different jobs every day. Should we throw a coming home party when you get back?" I asked laughing.

"That's just it, Caleb. Harry has been doing what he said. He's spending time on the Mount Fay and now he has decided he wants to spend some time at the ocean, too. I said a prayer that you wouldn't need him so we could go, I think he really needs more time."

I thought *maybe the mountain really does have powers,* as I answered Eunice, "Look Eunice, lets do it this way so he will not feel left out. Tell him as long as we have a number where we can leave him a message, he can go as long as he wants to."

"Thank you Caleb. I'm so glad you decided to come and work with us. I'll tell Harry what you said. God bless you. Goodbye."

It was two more weeks before Harry came back and he was a changed man. He even talked about maybe turning the company over to someone else to run. Eunice and I discussed this and thought that might not work for him, as he was too much of a control person to be able to stay out of the business.

I proposed that maybe little by little introducing the idea of selling the business outright would be a better avenue for him. That way he would have many more options of what he could do after he retired. He could well afford to do most anything since he had years of experience running his own business for over twenty years.

Shaq had been doing such a good job taking Harry's place, Harry convinced him to stay on as second in command. That gave Harry more free time and he and Eunice took frequent long weekend trips during good weather on his Indian Motorcycle. This was the same motorcycle he had the first time I saw him years ago. We would kid him and suggest it was time he bought one of those new Harleys.

He would say, "Quiet! That's sacrilege to any man who owns an Indian and if the rumors about a new Indian plant starting up are true, those Harleys are going to be left in the dust."

A couple of times they even rode all the way up to stay with Mother.

After the second time they went up, Eunice called when they got back, "Caleb, Jason was at Mother's and said he was going to be working close enough to Sterling to stay at Mother's. There is one draw back though, Jason has been living with an Asian girl for the last couple of years and we all realize that Mother would never allow that in her home. Jason has asked her to marry a couple of times but she always says maybe later. I encouraged him to be a little more aggressive next time because it would be such a good situation for the whole family with him living with Mother at the farm. I could see from my last visits Mother is not going to be able to carry on much longer there by herself. It might help if you wrote to Jason and tried to encourage him further."

It just so happened that Jason had called me worrying about Mother right after he stayed with her the last time he was there.

So I called him, "Jason, it's Caleb. Eunice just came back from Mother's and said you two talked about you moving back to the farm. I hope someday I can move back to Sterling, but it'll be a long time before that might happen."

"Life is funny, Caleb," Jason answered, "there I was when we were young talking about escaping Sterling and you were almost crying because you were leaving. My job keeps me moving a lot but I have a chance for more stationary position at my company's office just outside of Oscine. My girlfriend, Lea Lin has agreed to marry me and is quite excited at the prospect of living in the country. This isn't all tied with a bow yet, but I'm pretty sure that it all is going to happen. We even have discussed just having a simple wedding at the farm. Ask Eunice what she thinks about that. Lee Lin doesn't seem to care about a lot about making a big fuss about getting married and thinks getting married there would be fun. We know it will take a little subterfuge because we have always kept our living arrangements a secret from Mother. Hash this over with everyone and get back to me as soon as you can, Caleb," Jason ended as he said his goodbye.

It took another six months before Jason's job change came through but that worked out fine. Jason and Lea Lin were married at the farm about a month before his job change was scheduled and what a party it was. The whole family was able to make it for the first time since Dad's funeral and Mother was ecstatic to have us all there at once. It was plain to see that Mother and Lea Lin were going to be very happy with each other.

Mother was so happy about having us all together; that more than once she said, "I just know that Henry is looking down at this with a smile on his face."

Lea was going to have to give up her job to move with Jason. Jason had said she was happy about that because she really wanted to be free to explore country life. Though Jason's pay was more then adequate, Lea had enough talent as a florist to get another job any time if she got bored.

One by one my brothers and sisters and their families had to get back to their own lives and jobs; Mother asked if Jennie and I could stay a couple of more days hinting that there had been some progress in her and Jennie's project. Because Harry's company had biweekly paydays I couldn't stay any longer, but we made arrangements for Jennie and the children to stay.

Just before he left, my brother-in-law Aaron said, "Caleb let's take a walk."

As we walked through the enjoining woods, Aaron said, "Caleb I haven't heard a word about you doing any writing, have you given it all up?"

At first I started to say no but thinking about the question, I answered, "I haven't given it much thought, Aaron, but I guess I have to admit that I probably have, at least for the present. Still I plan to get back into writing someday, maybe after I retire."

Aaron said, "That's what I thought Caleb and why I asked you to walk with me. You certainly don't have to take any of my advice but I hope you will listen to what I believe is true. First of all, I have read some of your writings and some of your brother Josh's and I sense a thread of great ability in what I read. I know you have a very comfortable living working for Harry and that's all right. What isn't right is you not writing anything, not even for yourself. I predict that at some time in your life, you'll be writing again and you shouldn't allow yourself to get out of practice. You should have at least an article a month going whether it's published or not just to keep your ability alive."

"You know, Aaron," I answered, "One of the things I promised myself last time I was up on the mountain with my kids was that I would get back to writing, if only for their sake. The thought came to me after Janet asked me to recite some of Josh's writings about the mountain. Still life got in the way. Harry had problems and I had to give the job more time; you know how that is Aaron."

"What I know is that sometimes it's easier to find excuses than it is to make goals. One of the last things my father said to me before he died was that he was proud of the way I stuck to my goals and that he wished he had been more goal oriented in his life. I'm not putting you down Caleb, but Emma keeps showing me some of the things you and Josh had written and, like I said, I saw talent there and wanted to encourage you to keep writing," Aaron replied as we went back in.

I had to leave the next day and went back to Lynbrook by myself. I began to see some wisdom in Aaron's words so I sat down to write an article about Jason and his bride Lea and their farm wedding. I tore up paper after paper but it still felt good to be writing again. I hadn't realized what I had been missing. Jennie called about a week after I came back and said Mother and she were thinking about taking the children to see her folks before she came home. I told her I thought it should wait until I could be there too, she agreed and said they would be home in a week or ten days depending on the flights.

Chapter 7

With Harry back and Shaq working with him, things were going well at Jackstone Steel and since Harry hadn't bid on any new jobs, my work schedule was easy enough so I could write during office hours.

Shaq was worried about Harry not bidding on new jobs. He was afraid they would have to let men go when some of the contracts were finished. Harry told him not to worry that he had been looking at new jobs even if he hadn't bid. He didn't want the company to get bigger than it was, but would bid enough jobs to keep the crews he had.

Shaq had been trying to get us to get together with his and Etta's families for a cookout. Jennie and I had talked about it, so about a week after she and the children got back from Sterling we went to Etta's house on a Sunday afternoon. I hadn't seen Etta since her wedding and though she had four children and had put on some weight she still was a striking woman.

We had a grand time and so did our children. We talked about old times and how they had forced me to take them and Joan to my job site and how I was teased about my harem. We all wondered what had happened with Norman and Virginia and I promised I would inquire about them next time I was in Sterling.

Jennie told them I was writing again and Etta said she had wondered about that when she heard I was coming back to work for Harry.

Finally Tom, Etta's husband, broke in saying, "Come on, Caleb, and Shaq, let's take a walk. Maybe if we get a way from these women for a while, we can tell some stories that Caleb can use in his writing."

Realizing our conversations had kind of left him out, I answered. "Great idea, Tom. I know its good journalism to hear stories from people who you are just getting to know."

After we left the women, most of the talk was about k work. I knew Shaq had brought Tom with him when he decided to come back to Jackstone Steel but since I very seldom went out on the job sites, I never got to know him. Listening to him and Shaq as we walked I came to see how well Etta had chosen.

As we rejoined the women, Jennie said, "Well Caleb, did you get stories that you can use in your writing?"

Tom laughed, slapping me on the back said, "After he told us all about being a harem master, we didn't have any stories to compete with him. By the way, Etta how come you let him get away?"

At first I thought, here comes trouble but Etta just laughed saying, "After spending time in Sterling and seeing all his country girls and meeting Jennie, I knew I didn't have a chance so I came back to Oklahoma and found you. While you three have been gone, Jennie has been catching us up on life with Caleb and I'm sure made the right choice."

Loraine, Shaq's wife said, "Tell us, Caleb, is it true that Jennie had to rope and tie you to get you out of Sterling?"

"Okay, that's it," I shouted, trying to sound angry, "It has been over twenty years since I left Sterling and I thought I had left this kind of harassment behind. I'm not sure why it is that every time a group from my past gets together it becomes *picking on Caleb day*. No, it wasn't a rope that got me up to New York with Jennie, it was something much more seductive than that."

Shaq and Tom, almost in unison, said, "Yeah! Let's hear about it, Jennie."

"Oh! There isn't much to tell really," Jennie chimed in, "but one thing for sure, it wasn't seduction. With the likes of Joan, Betty and Etta and their looks to compete with, I didn't stand a chance. It's just that working with

Caleb way back when we were young, I realized he needed saving from himself and made that my lifetime priority. There have been a few times since I reeled him in that I wasn't too sure of what I caught. All and all though, he has worked out kind of nicely despite his sordid past."

It was getting late and I was worried about Jennie's answer starting more discussions about the past that were better not spoken, I said, "I hate to break up such a wonderful afternoon but we really should be getting back home and getting the children down. We should do this again at our house soon but without any more Caleb history."

As we said our goodbyes, Loraine said with a laugh, "Oh, that's too bad Caleb, I was saving the stories about your Oklahoma dance hall days for next time."

As we drove off Jennie said, "You shouldn't get upset with the joking Caleb, after all you do have a colored past. You don't have to be afraid on my account at what will come out."

"Probably not, Jennie," I answered, "but how about Tom, Shaq and our children?"

There was something about discussions with old friends that brought back memories of the things I used to write about. I wrote an article about how it was back when men who did the logging lived in shanties that moved from job to job. Much to my surprise the second magazine that I sent it to accepted it. They required some rewriting but still it was exciting to have my writing published again. Jennie encouraged me to keep using past memories in my writing. Over the next couple of years I was successful in placing several such pieces.

We had been able to get back to Sterling a couple of times a year to visit the last several years. Because of Mother's insistence, Jennie, I, and the children went for a few controlled visits to her family.

Lea, Jason's wife had taken to country life and rejuvenated the vegetable garden and was raising a few sheep. Mother seemed very happy that the farm was producing again but voted down Jason's suggestion that they get a cow. She felt confident she could manage a few sheep when Jason and Lea went away for a few days but a cow would be too much for her.

The children and I hiked Mount Fay every chance we got. Trips there seemed to spur memories to write about. Though I was building a sizable portfolio of memory pieces, it was hard to find suitable markets for many of them, although it was fun recalling and writing again.

Because Janet and Josh both had come down with some strange virus, we had missed this year's scheduled fall visit to Sterling before school started. Janet was in her last year of high school and Josh was a junior this year, and we promised mother we would be down first school break.

We were in the process of making arrangements to go around their school schedule when I received a call from Jason.

He was pretty upset saying, "Caleb you have to get down here right away. Jennie too, but don't bring the children."

"Come on. Jason, you know I need more than that to drop everything up here and come running, what's up?" I asked quietly.

"It's pretty bad Caleb, Jennie's dad is dead and it looks like Arnie shot him. Mother was at their house when it happened. I had a hell of a time convincing the police to let Mother come home but Arnie is still in jail, maybe forever."

Telling Jason we would be there the next day, I called Jennie and told her that her dad had died and that we should go down. She was hesitant at first about the children. I told her I would call Eunice and see if she would stay at our house with them and that we would be back in a couple of days.

The next day as we flew down, Jennie said, "How did he die Caleb?"

I decided she should know the truth or at least as much of it as I knew, so I said. "Jason said your dad was shot and the police are holding Arnie."

"Oh My God! All these years and it finally has happened. Both of the boys have threatened to shoot him more then once. Poor Arnie, we have to help him, Caleb," she said crying on my shoulder.

"We'll do everything we can for him, Jennie," I answered wondering how much we could do.

Lea picked us up at the airport outside of Oscin.

She said, "Jason has contacted a lawyer and he says we should not talk to anyone about what has happened until all the facts are garnered. Jason said I wasn't to tell you anything yet, he wants us all to be together for Mother to tell what happened."

As we gathered at the farm, Mother looked like she had aged ten years since I had seen her.

She said, "This is so hard. I keep hoping I'm going to wake up and find this is just a nightmare. Yesterday morning I was by the Sledge house so thought I would drop in and say hi. Nobody was home except your father, Jennie, and he said, 'Out slumming Mrs. Carney?' I could see he had been drinking so I decided to leave, just as I turned to leave Arnie came in. Your father said, 'Have you met my cur of a son yet Mrs. Carney or doesn't that whore master son of yours allow him to visit? You see this family isn't like the mighty Carney home. No, my oldest daughter Janet runs away, then your son helps Jennie run away so he can have her all to himself some place up in New York. Then my oldest son Arthur goes away and gets himself killed, now all we have left is this little cur who creeps back to see us once in a great while.'"

"Arnie put his arm on your dad and said, 'Come on Father, that's enough.' Your dad was old but he must have been still be pretty strong because when Arnie turned to me and said, 'Pay no attention Mrs. Carney, it's just the drink." Your dad hit him on the side of the head so hard he staggered across the room and fell through a door. I started towards Arnie to see if he was alright and your dad was screaming, 'Get out, get out, we don't need your kind around here.'"

"Then raising his hand he came towards me. Suddenly there was a big bang and he slumped to the floor like a sack of grain and there was blood everywhere. Arnie was standing in the doorway with a rifle in his hands. I started screaming. Arnie said, 'Just leave, Mrs. Carney. Call the cops and make sure that my mother doesn't come back here.'"

"Some one walking by heard the shot and me screaming and came running in. They took one look and ran off, and soon there were State Police all over the place. They took Arnie and me to the police barracks in Oscin. I called Jason who came and talked them into letting me go home, but they kept your brother. Jason went to your house to check on your mother; the police had your house cordoned off. Your mother was with a neighbor and didn't want to see Jason. He checked this morning and your father's body has been moved to a funeral home but no one can enter the house yet."

Jennie sat in silence for several minutes after mother spoke, remembering her deep depression after losing the baby I was worried but she finally spoke saying. "I'm terribly sorry you had to go through that mother Carney, my family has always been headed for some kind of catastrophe but nobody outside of the family could have imagined this. Caleb, we have to see if we can contact Janet, then we'll go to see Arnie if they let us. After that we should see about arranging father's burial."

Lea said, "Jennie if you have an address, I'll get on the phone and see if I can locate Janet for you. It might pay you to talk to the lawyer that Jason contacted before you see Arnie. I know it's a lot to think about but whatever is going to happen to Arnie, we don't want to make it worse by making a mistake now."

Jennie gave Lea a little hug saying, "I'm glad Jason found you Lea, not just because of now but for all you have done to make life in the Carney family so much easier."

It didn't take Lea long to get in touch with Janet and she said she could be here the next morning. We called the lawyer that Jason had talked to and he said that he had been to see Arnie and that he had already confessed to the murder. He felt that he was going to be a little out of his league with this case and advised us find a good criminal lawyer. He did advise that we should offer nothing to the police without advice from such a lawyer.

I called Richard, Hester's husband for advice; I knew he had dealt with lawyers in his company and would be able to help us.

After I told him what had happened, he said, "Give me a couple of days Caleb, I'll see what I can do."

We went to the barracks in Oscin to see Arnie; he was a real broken man. Jennie held him for a minute while asking if we could have some privacy.

The sergeant on duty said, "I don't see a reason why not."

Arnie said, "I'm so sorry Jennie, I don't know how it happened. When Dad hit me, I landed in the other room and the gun was right beside the door. I never had a conscious thought about shooting him. I saw him going after Caleb's mother and the next thing I know, he's laying on the floor with a hole in his head with your mother screaming bloody murder and I'm sitting on the floor holding a gun. I know I'm going to jail for life or worse but don't fret Jennie, life has never been that precious for me anyway. I know we haven't been in contact but I have always been proud of what you have done with your life; I wish I had been strong enough to get away from the family."

Jennie said, "Don't take all the blame on yourself Arnie, families like ours have a way of destroying life. Now no more confessing anything to the police. We are going to get you a lawyer who understands these kinds of things before we make any decisions about what to do."

"What's going to happen to Mother, Jennie?" Arnie asked miserably, as we were leaving about two hours later. "You know she isn't capable of living on her own, as much of a terror Dad was, he did keep the house running and the bills paid."

"We don't have an answer yet Arnie but Caleb and I will go see her and when Janet gets here we'll make sure an arrangement is made so she is safe and comfortable," Jennie answered, as she hugged Arnie goodbye.

Outside Jennie said, "I think we should take care of Dad's arrangements before we see Mom. I didn't want to mention it to Arnie; it would just upset him more. I think we need to know what will be happening before we see Mother, I'm sure she'll be asking."

I hadn't given Jennie's mother much thought, the few times I had seen her she had never talked much and it was plain to see she was subjected to her husband. Now I wondered if there wasn't more of a problem than that.

At the funeral parlor, Jennie was curt and to the point selecting cremation and the very minimum being offered, with no services except a brief one at the cemetery. Like all long-time Sterling residents, they already had a plot were Arthur's ashes and Veteran's stone were placed.

When we finally located the neighbor were Jennie's mother was supposed to be, we were told she had been taken to the hospital. Jennie was inconsolable on the way to the hospital.

She kept repeating, "My father shot and killed, my brother in jail and my mother in the hospital, I deserted them all."

I decided it was better not to say anything until just before we arrived at the hospital, then I said, "Okay, Jennie, you have to get a grip on yourself. No matter what you feel, if we are going to be of any help to anyone, you are going to be needed. If anyone deserted, I think it was your father who deserted the family long, long ago. There wasn't any way that you or your siblings could have change things. Try remembering what Arnie said about wishing he had been strong enough to leave. Knowing you like I do, I can imagine that could just as well be you sitting there in that jail."

"You're right, Caleb. There were many times I wished he was dead and under the same circumstances, I probably would have done the same thing as Arnie did. I just needed to get those thoughts out in the open; I think I'm ready to face Mother's problem now." She dried her eyes.

In the hospital we were shown to her room. What a shock! Jennie's mother was on life support and was strapped to the bed, both of her arms were in bandages and though she seemed awake we couldn't get a response from her.

We hadn't been able to find out in Sterling why she went to the hospital. At the desk they told us that she had came in with both wrist slashed in an apparent suicide attempt. They contributed her lack of response to the medication she was on and the restraints were mandatory for suspected suicides. Jennie and I spent a couple of hours with her but were told it probably would be another several hours before she would be conscious enough to talk. So getting a promise they would call us, we left.

The next day Janet arrived and insisted that the Carneys didn't have to get involved, that this was a Sledge family problem and she and Jennie would handle it.

Mother said, "Now Janet, I know this kind of thing is a shock and things sometimes get said that shouldn't. I need you to understand that Jennie is as much a Carney as a Sledge and therefore we are all family. You have to remember that young Janet and Josh are carrying both bloods and whatever happens, we want them to be proud of what their Carney side does in this situation."

Jennie said, "Janet has always been the one in the family that we always turned too, Mother Carney. She couldn't know how good a family we have all become. Give her a little time to adjust to the fact that she doesn't have to be my protector anymore. Caleb will go with Janet and me as we visit Arnie and Mother. I'm sure by the time she spends some time with us she will understand we are all family."

At the hospital Jennie's mother was conscious but incoherent, when we left an hour later both the girls were in tears.

Janet said, "Lord what are we going to do, Jennie? She will never be able to survive without someone with her; I can't take her with me and I am never going to come back to Sterling to live."

Jennie just cried harder, so I said, "Look, as bad as this is I'm sure that we will find a solution to your mother's situation. I think what we need to do right now is concentrate on Arnie. After you girls pull yourselves together I think we should go see him. I don't believe that they will keep him much longer in Oscin and we should see him as often as they will let us."

In Oscin we stopped in for some coffee to give us all a chance to talk before seeing Arnie. We spend about an hour going over different scenarios before it dawned on us that there were so many ifs in our thoughts that our discussions were not going to be useful.

Finally Janet said, "Caleb, you mentioned a lawyer. Do we actually have one yet?"

"Only as an adviser, but my sister's husband, who has connections, is looking for one that he thinks will be able to really help Arnie." I answered.

As we were leaving the restaurant, Janet, putting her hand on my shoulder, said, "I'm sorry, Caleb, for how I acted with your mother. I hope she can forgive me. I can see now how wonderful it is for Jennie to be a part of your family."

"You don't have to worry about Mother Carney, Janet," Jennie answered. "She is the most understanding women I have ever met and you can say the same for all Caleb's family. They will always be there for each other and any member or friend of the family, too."

When we got to the barracks, Arnie was still uncertain how it all could have happened and talked incessantly about it.

Janet consoled him saying, "Arnie, don't blame yourself. All of us have been angry enough to kill father many times. It's hard to believe it was you because you were the most passive of all of us."

"So many times I fought being angry with Father, telling myself he probably couldn't help it. Since Arthur has been gone he has treated me worse then he did his dogs, always calling me his cur. I wouldn't have ever gone back to the house except that I worried about what would happen to Mother if I didn't stop in once in a while to give his anger an outlet."

Arnie paused for a moment in deep thought, then said, "You know that was probably it, when I saw him going after Mrs. Carney, my fears about Mother made all the anger I have been fighting for years just blow up in me, without me even realizing it."

Janet held him in her arms, while Jennie told him we were getting him a good lawyer and not to get down on himself. We stayed with Arnie until we noticed the sergeant on duty getting nervous.

As we left he said, "We will keep him here as long as we can but when he goes to the state facilities you won't be allowed to touch him or be entirely alone with him, at least at first."

We thanked the sergeant and went back to Sterling. Janet wanted to go to her parent's house but she wasn't allowed in. The police on duty said it would probably be another day before we would be able to enter.

When we got home I went to look up one of Josh's poems that had come to mind while I was listening to Arnie. Finally, I found the one I was looking for. It was called: *Anger's Curse.*

Like gladiators of old, who to the arena fell
He stood in jealous throes, suffering the pains of hell
As the hot red blood of anger through his body cruised
The crowd stood wildly shouting, turn the animal loose
But well he knew the consequence; he had felt this way before
The wild uncontrollable animal, would just leave blood and gore

But the horde kept right on calling, our need you can't refuse
As they stood there wildly shouting, turn the animal loose
The cry became demanding, from the crowd escapes a sigh
The animal eludes him now; blood and guts will fly
The battle is short and bloody, the crowds no longer muse
They sit in fearful silence; they just saw the animal loose

Two days later, I got a call from Richard saying he had located two lawyers who would be great for Arnie, but they were very expensive. He said he had talked to Aaron about helping out with the expenses. He was willing but he wanted to talk to a lawyer he worked with first.

That night Aaron called. He was pretty excited saying, "Guess what, Caleb! One of the partners in my company was a was a court appointed lawyer when he first started out and later worked for a law firm that dealt in criminal law. He has often said nothing got his blood flowing like a challenging criminal case. When I was inquiring about lawyers he came to me with a proposition."

"He said he would like to look into the case and if it looked winnable he would work pro-bono as long as he could get the company name mentioned as supplying the lawyer. He needs to get some papers signed so he can go see Arnie as his lawyer and would like to talk to the rest of the family before deciding to take it on. I have heard a lot of good things about this man, Caleb, and if he thinks there is a chance, this is the way to go."

I thanked Aaron and said I would get back to him as soon as I had talked it over with Janet and Jennie.

Janet was skeptical of someone wanting to do something for nothing saying. "One of the things I have found out in life is that if it is to good to be true it usually isn't. What do we know about this man, what motivates him to want to do something like this?"

Jennie said, "I don't know about the lawyer but I do know about Aaron and he is as true blue and honest as they come. I say we should meet this man and then decide."

"I'll tell you what, Janet, if it will make you feel better," I jumped in, not wanting to lose the offer. "I'll ask Richard to check him out. Richard has a lot of contacts among lawyers and can ask for opinions about him if that would make you more comfortable."

A couple of days after I called Richard, he called back saying, "You have a winner there Caleb! Nothing but good reports have cone back about him. All I got to say if he is doing this pro-bono, it's a gift worth thousands of dollars."

After thanking Richard I talked to Janet and Jennie and then called Aaron and told him to set up a meeting. Aaron called right back saying the lawyer wanted to meet with Arnie and the family right away to evaluate the case so we'd have time to get someone else in case he doesn't feel it's right for him.

The next day Aaron set up a meeting in Oscin in an office they had available to his company.

On the way to the meeting Jennie said, "Do you think there is any special way we should handle this Caleb?"

"I think we will be answering questions most of the time and we have to be honest no matter how embarrassing or difficult the questions may seem. I had a chance to watch lawyers work when I worked for the newspaper, and it always seemed they questioned, questioned, questioned until the found something that they could work their case with."

Aaron was at the office and introduced us to the lawyer, Mr. Donald Langley. After the introductions he asked us to sit down and motioned for Aaron to leave.

Then he said, "First of all, forget the mister and call me Don; now I know how hard these kinds of interviews can be, but if you stick with me I'll make this as short as I can. First I need one of you to tell me the facts, as you know them. No background yet, just the story of the actual incident."

Janet looked at Jennie said, "I think it's best that Caleb tells you as we might be to emotional. It was his mother who was there when it happened."

I told Don the story just the way Mother had told us, only adding that so far Arnie has no recall of grabbing the gun or shooting, though he realizes he must have.

We spent the next two hours answering questions and though sometimes the girls were close to tears revealing their home life, I credited them for being so brave. Don reassured them constantly that none of this would ever leave that room without their consent. As they talked I could see Don's interest building and had a good feeling about him.

When we left we went to the barracks to see Arnie. We met him as a group.

As soon as Arnie seemed comfortable with Don, Don asked us to leave saying, "Find a coffee shop or something, we might be a while."

At the coffee shop, both Janet and Jennie said how impressed they were with Don and for the first time felt that there might be some hope.

Don joined us about an hour after we left him and said, "I have decided to take the case. I need you to understand that I will be mentioning the company's name as often as it seems reasonable. That way I can justify taking this pro-bono case to my partners. Though I have a few ideas they are better left unsaid because I need much more information than I have now to make a judgment on how to proceed. I will be talking to the police and attorney general's office and will need you to sign papers to show that I have been retained to represent Arnie."

After signing the necessary papers and thanking Don we went back to the farm. Janet said she had to find a place to stay and make some calls to her boss to arrange a leave.

When Mother heard this she said, "Young lady, you are to stay right here with family. Not only do we have plenty of room but this is where the lawyer and police will be contacting whoever is needed."

Janet said, "Thank you Mrs. Carney. I was hoping that would be possible. I want to be as close to Jennie as long as I can. After spending time with your Caleb and seeing how well you function as a family, I know how wrong I was to challenge you like I did."

"Don't give that another thought, Janet," Mother answered, "We all understand the pressure you were under and after all we were practically strangers to you when you first came. Caleb told me about your mother, I had a chance to visit with her a couple of times before this all happened so when you think it's alright, I would like to visit her again at the hospital."

We spent everyday for the next couple of weeks visiting Arnie and his mother.

Don called us pretty near everyday. He informed us he was able to convince them not to transfer Arnie to the county jail and that he was going before a judge using Arnie's medical discharge papers to try to get him entered into a ninety day evaluation program at a hospital. He warned us not to read too much into that, it just that he thought it was better for Arnie than being confined in the county jail and it might help at a trial.

The girls had finally been able to communicate with their mother and she told them that after she heard her husband had been killed and Arnie had been arrested for it, she felt so alone and scared she slit her wrists. She apologized over and over again saying it wouldn't have happened if she had known her girls were coming.

As glad as we all were she was at least coherent, the girls started to feel guilty after listening to her.

They became very worried about how they were going to take care her. Finally Jennie said, "Caleb I know how much I'm asking, but is it possible for us to take mother back with us? If it is going to be long-term, we can afford to build on a couple of rooms for her."

I had already thought about that possibility and as much as it worried me, I knew we didn't have many options. So I answered, "Jennie your mother is family and if that's what you want, I'm sure we can handle it. The children are old enough now to understand that it is the right thing for us to do."

113

Eunice called and we talked to the children. They both asked how much longer we would be before we came home. Eunice said Harry had managed to get out the last pay roll but hoped I got back before another one came up because he knew the books weren't quite right without me there.

The hospital wanted to release Jennie's mother but said she wasn't able to be on her own.

Mother, who had been visiting her, said, "There isn't any reason she can't stay here until you girls have another solution."

At first Janet was against that saying, "Look, we can't ask any more of you Mrs. Carney, it just isn't right."

Mother answered, "I tell you what Janet. Why don't you call me Mother Carney? That way you'll get used to the idea that we are all family and you don't have to keep fighting us about being involved."

Janet went over, hugged Mother and completely broke down crying on her shoulder saying, "Mother Carney, nothing would make me prouder then being a member of your family. Still my family has been such a disaster, I'm not sure I would know how to be a part of one like yours."

Mother held Janet saying, "You just made the first move, Janet, by accepting us. We can make a room for your mother in the parlor. We hardly ever use that room. That's where Henry stayed when he was laid up after his accident, so we are used to that being used as a sick room."

Mrs. Sledge came out of the hospital a few days after that. She thought she was going back to her own home and was a hand full at our house for a couple of days until Mother, Lea and her daughters were able to finally calm her down.

After she settled down, she seemed capable of taking care of herself, even to the extent of changing her own bandages and caring for her wounds. She even joined Lea in the garden and helped in caring for the animals.

The change in her even amazed Jennie, who said, "I can hardly believe that is my mother! She actually seems happy. I don't think I have ever seen her really happy before"

Don called and said he had been successful in getting Arnie into a hospital for ninety days, warning us visiting would be more limited there. He also said not to expect to see any court case for a year or two.

He said he needed to question us again and wondered if Arnie's mother would be available too. I told him it had to be soon as I needed to get back to Oklahoma, so we made arrangements to meet at the farm the next day.

Don spent a couple of hours with Mother Sledge the next day and surprisingly it seemed to have gone well. At least it didn't seem to have any adverse effects on her.

Jennie had her father cremated and we had been waiting to hold burial services until her mother was ready.

Jennie wanted to have the services before I left but Janet said, "I don't care when you have the services. I am not going to go anyway."

When Mother heard this she said, "You know, Janet, life has its way of scarring all of us, but the worse scars to have to live with are the ones we cause ourselves. No matter how hard it is for you to go now, I believe you will have harder regrets from not going later on."

Janet held Mother's hand and said, "Mother Carney, if that is what you believe, I have to believe you and go. Thank you for seeing through my anger and confusion. I have spent so many years trying to pretend I didn't have a family. It has become a habit to think like that."

Two days later we held a short service at the cemetery. I knew that Jennie and Janet had talked to the pastor and didn't know what to expect from him. The funeral parlor had set up a podium next to the grave and where he took his place, he said, "Let us each reach for God in a silent prayer."

I was wondering if this was all there was going to be when he started speaking. "Lord, look down up on us, help us to understand the ununderstandable. Lord, I have been advised not to pray for this man's soul because it was assumed he didn't have one. I personally cannot accept that Lord, so help my thoughts as we say goodbye to Orin Sledge's earthly remains. My belief, Lord, is that you are the master of all, yet sometimes it is hard to understand why some things happen under your watch. This man seemingly led a life of boiling anger, scarring many of those who were around him, some so bad that they believe he has no soul. I cannot believe that, Lord. Let his life show others not to live in anger like he did. Now Lord we return Orin back to you praying that you will be with us all in understanding and healing. Amen"

As Mother went over to the pastor, Janet and Jennie both joined her in thanking him for his understanding. Their mother, who had been very quiet during the service, stood over Orin's urn shedding tears silently. The pastor went over and said a little prayer just for her and Mother went over to help her as she started to leave the grave.

Aaron, Emma, Richard, Hester and Jason were at the services. Lea had begged off saying she would stay at the farm and prepare something for the reception after the services. It was great to have so many of the family home despite the occasion. Janet and I were both going to have to leave the next day.

At the end of the day, Janet came to me and said, "Caleb, Jennie is so lucky to have you and your family. For the first time I can remember I'm going to be sad about leaving Sterling. I know Jennie is planning on taking our mother to Oklahoma. Thank you for that and I will get down there to visit and will help with her expenses. Caleb, could you ever have imagined this way back when we all worked at Muldons?"

"No Janet, but I do believe a seed was planted back then that made all this possible and I couldn't imagine life without Jennie." I answered giving her a hug.

The next day Janet and I left Sterling, me back to Oklahoma and Janet back to her life. As I thought about it on the plane I didn't know where or what, it had never been mentioned.

Chapter 8

The children were happy to have me back when I arrived home in Oklahoma. It seems that Eunice was more of a strict disciplinarian than I was.

Janet was especially interested in what had happened, her Nellyism had picked up on Arnie being troubled way back when we had met him that day on the mountain. I explained as much as I thought a high school senior should know.

Eunice had asked me if she should tell them why we had left in such a rush, so Janet already knew the basics of what had happened. I filled in Janet about Jennie's mother, and explained to both her and Josh that Grandma Sledge would probably come to stay with us. I explained about Arnie and his lawyer and how he hoped to get Arnie free or least a light sentence. Josh accepted this nonplused but Janet was fully animated by all that had happened, especially the part of my having been with her namesake Aunt Janet.

It occurred to me then how it must seem strange to my children that they had little chance to know Jennie's family and had never met Janet or Arthur. As my daughter went on and on with her questions and theories, it made me think more and more of how much she was like Nellie. I suddenly realized that she also had only met Homer and Nellie fleetingly at Dad's funeral when she was much younger. I made a mental note to try to remedy that as soon as I got a chance.

Nellie who had joined the Peace Corps when it started in 1961 and was now traveling the world with her husband serving as ambassadors for peace for the United Nations. Homer was seldom in Sterling and almost never at the same time we were. I was especially interested in Janet and Nellie having a talk about Janet's extra perceptivity that she seemed to have inherited from Nellie.

A couple of weeks after I was home, Jennie called wanting some help in making some decisions. They had received an offer for the Sledge property and after much discussion with her mother and Arnie and Janet, they had decided selling it was probably the best thing to do. Their problem was that both Arnie and his mother wanted some things kept from the house. What Arnie wanted didn't cause a problem but her mother wanted to keep most of her furniture and Jennie definitely didn't want to bring any of it to Oklahoma.

Knowing Jennie's mother's condition still had to be a big part of our decisions; I suggested that there probably was some place in the barn where her furniture could be stored. A couple of nights later Jennie called thanking me for the suggestion, saying Jason had arranged everything for her.

She had talked to her mother about moving to Oklahoma with us and her mother had cried and cried. Her mother said if she couldn't stay on the farm then she would use the house money to find a place to stay in Sterling. My mother told Jennie in private that if her family thought that staying on the farm was best, it probably could be worked out. Jennie told me she couldn't do that to my family, it wasn't fair. I told her to let the idea be tossed around for a while. I suggested perhaps she should come back for a couple of weeks to be with the children and we could discuss what we wanted for an addition to the house.

When I went to pick Jennie up at the airport, I was surprised at how tired and worn she looked.

On the way to the house she said. "I'm not sure that making my mother come here is the right thing to do, Caleb. She is adamant that she isn't leaving Sterling; she wants to find a place close to Lea and your mother so she can still work around the farm. I don't think there is anything close enough for her to be able to walk back and forth. I'm afraid we made a mistake in selling her house. I think at the time we sold the idea of selling to my mother, she thought she would be staying at the farm. It is such a mess Caleb, I feel so bad we can't let her stay. Mother has been the happiest I have ever seen her living there."

I put my arm on Jennie saying, "Let's drop all the troubles for a while. You have two wonderful children waiting for you at home who need to be assured everything is going to be all right. I'll have Jason do a little research about a place for your mother in Sterling but I think we should prepare for her to be with us eventually. We can go along with her idea at least for now. If it doesn't work out, then it'll be easier to convince her to come stay with us, after she isn't at the farm."

"You know, Caleb," Jennie said patting me on the knee. "It seems as though the whole Carney family has a way of finding solutions no matter what the problem."

"It's my mother's way of thinking that has rubbed off on us but I wouldn't lean too much on my having as good answers as hers." I said laughing.

Janet and Josh had worked hard to have the house all shined up when their mother came home and Jennie was thrilled at all they had done. Jennie spent the next week resting and catching up with what our children had been up to.

I avoided talking about Sterling until after she had been home for few weeks. When I called Jason about finding a place for my mother-in-law he laughed saying, "Where have you been hiding, Caleb? It's all settled here. Lea is thrilled to have her here and she is wonderful company for Mother. I see it as a win-win situation for all of us. I did have some concern at first but she is so demure, sometimes it's like she isn't even here. I'm not aware of how she was before but she seems so content now I wouldn't want to take that away from anyone, especially someone her age."

"Jason I'm not sure we can sell this to Janet but I know Jennie has had a fear that moving her here would defeat all the gains she has made since leaving the hospital. I think I should discuss this with Mother, is she there?" I asked.

Mother got on the phone saying, "Caleb I've been listening to Jason and though we haven't told Jean yet, all of us have discussed it thoroughly and if the Sledge's don't object, we want to make it official."

"Mother, I think you have just made Jennie one very happy woman. She knew how much her mother wanted to stay there; she just didn't think it was fair to our family. I don't know about Arnie but Jennie will call Janet right away and get back to you." I answered excitingly.

"About Arnie, Lea is taking Jean to see him tomorrow. I think I will go with them to help reassure him we want her to stay." Mother answered before saying goodbye.

When I talked to Jennie she just sat there looking at me strangely before she said, "Caleb, I have prayed for an answer but I never dared pray it would be this, as much as I wanted it to be. Are you sure about this, it seems much to good to be true?"

"I talked Jason and Mother and it isn't only that they are trying to do something nice, they really want her to stay. Seems that she not only works the farm but it also makes life fuller for Mother, having her to talk to. Now you get on the phone to Janet and don't let her talk you out of it." I answered.

Janet had her usual objections that the Carneys shouldn't be carrying the Sledge problems but after Jennie explained how much happier her mother was at the farm and how she had cried about having to move to Oklahoma, she relented and okayed the arrangement.

The next night Jennie called to tell Mother about Janet and to see how Arnie took it.

After the call Jennie came to me and said, "I married into a wonderful family, Caleb. I just wish I had let myself get to know them sooner. Arnie was so happy that he cried and your mother held him even though the attendant objected, saying, 'he is my son I have a right.' You know your mother has even reached Janet, who has made a practice of shutting people out of her life."

Late that night as we lay in bed I got to thinking about Janet. I asked Jennie, "Just what is it that Janet does for a living and how come we never hear anything about a man in her life? I know many of the Sterling boys thought she was very attractive, but I never heard about her dating any of them, though I know she and Josh used to spend some time together?"

Jennie was quiet for a moment and then said, "Janet works in the sales office of a big cosmetic company and has a really good position. As for a man,

Caleb, she doesn't have one in her life, though she has a female companion. Now Caleb, this has to stay just between you and me. If and when Janet wants the family to know she's gay, she will tell them. I have always known growing up that Janet and I were different when it came to boys. I didn't really know how far it went until right after our Janet was born. I anguished over having chosen her name for our daughter when I found out but over the years I have gotten over it. I hope this isn't going to make you want to alienate my sister from our family."

"I wouldn't worry about that, Jennie," I answered. "If I have any worries about our Janet, it's that she seems to have inherited my sister Nellie's uncanny ability to sense what people are feeling."

"Thank you, Caleb, for being understanding," Jennie, said, holding me close. "I'm aware of Janet's sixth sense and have always told her that she should see it as a gift from God and only use it as He would want it used. She told me how when she first met Arnie she could feel how troubled he was. I wondered at that time if I should come clean about my dysfunctional family and see if we could help him but I decided we didn't need that burden, now I wonder."

"Don't do that to yourself, Jennie," I exclaimed worriedly. "I started on that trip when George was mangled by the bull. What if I had grabbed him or if I had grabbed the rope. Our pastor explained that if I hadn't personally and intentionally caused the harm then I didn't have responsibility. I relied heavily on those words when Dad got hurt. At first I felt if I had stayed working with him he wouldn't have had the accident that crippled him. I know now that no amount of recrimination can change what has already happened. Mother has always said we should pray for the strength to deal with what is, not waste our strength on what could have or should have been."

Since it had been settled about Jennie's mother. Jennie decided she didn't need to go back unless she was needed for Arnie's case. We decided if everything went well we would wait until our usual spring visit to go back. We were able to stay advised about Arnie's case through Jason and Aaron who saw Arnie's lawyer often.

Arnie was moved from the hospital to a minimum-security prison. The prison was too far away from Sterling for his mother or Jennie to make regular visits but Janet said she would be able to get there at least once a month. Jason said he would try to find a way Jean could make the trip to visit but he hadn't got it worked out yet. Jennie found a flight that would take her close to the prison and made plans to fly down for a weekend. Our Janet asked if she could go with her mother. At first we said no, but after talking it over, we relented.

Because of Arnie's record, the prison guards let Jennie and Janet spend considerable time with him when they flew down. Despite Janet's stream of questions, Arnie took a liking to her and seemed to enjoy her probing.

On their second visit Janet asked, "Has the lawyer, Mr. Langley, done anything for you yet, Arnie?"

Arnie laughed saying, "You really cut right to the case, don't you missy? They are letting me call Don at least once a week. He has always kept me well informed. Right now he is trying out different scenarios, as he calls them, before deciding what will be the best approach for my defense. He told me that it might be possible to force them to set bail but at this time it would be prohibitively high. His idea is, in all probability I will have to serve some time and he may be able to get a verdict that will get me off with time served."

"There are several different ways that manslaughter can be considered and he is arguing each one among his peers to see which one looks the best. He has also talked to me about justifiable homicide, he believes he could make a good case of that but it would put my mother, Aunt Janet, and your mother on the stand and I don't want that. I am comfortable here at this prison and even if I never get free again, I'm going to be all right."

Jennie who had listened quietly said. "Arnie, if Don thinks justifiable homicide is your best chance, that's the way we should go. I'm sure Janet and I could live through it."

"I couldn't do that to any of you, Jennie." Arnie answered. "Think what that would mean. All that you have been hiding and running away from would be spread all over the newspapers. I'm sure Janet doesn't want the life she lives to become an open book to the public. The last thing we want is the complete Sledge history to become a saga for the whole world to leer about. Even if you and Janet agreed to take the stand, think of what that might do to Mother."

"Don is coming down here next month and he believes he will have a strategy to talk over with me. Jason sends messages about Mother through

Don when I call him. Isn't it great about her finding happiness at the farm? You sure married right Jennie. I always liked Caleb; I never told anyone before but he was with me when I shot that wildcat. You know the one that Mr. Banner had stuffed and kept at the Sterling Inn displayed along side of Caleb's big trout?"

After hearing all this Janet was beside herself with questions.

Luckily for Arnie, visiting time was almost over and Jennie said, "No more questions Janet. We can discuss all of this later. I don't want to spend our last few minutes with Arnie with him being cross examined by you."

Arnie laughed and said. "It might be good for me, Jennie. She probes like a lawyer and I might need the practice before this is through."

"Well, if you really feel that way, maybe I should bring her again. I had half decided that bringing her here was a bad idea. What we need to know Arnie, is what we can get for you before we leave and what you would like any of us to send you." Jennie asked seriously.

"I don't need much here, Jennie," Arnie answered with a shrug of his shoulders. "Aaron has set a fund up at the prison I'm allowed to draw on if I need anything. There is one thing though; most of the guys here have some pictures from their families or from some of favorite time in their lives. I'm not sure what I want, but pictures of Mother and my two sisters would be good. And discussing the old days made me kind of want to have something like a picture of my cat at the Inn, if there is one around. I had several that Mr. Banner had given me, but Dad tore them up long ago. I should have known enough to hide them but I kept them on the wall of my room."

"Mr. Banner is gone now but I believe that the Inn is being run by a relative of his and I'm sure they will still have those pictures somewhere. I will contact Jason as soon as we get back and have him check." Jennie answered as she kissed Arnie goodbye.

Jennie and Janet left from the prison to go right to the airport where they just had time for a lunch before taking off.

Janet was bursting with curiosity from all that she had heard but Jennie put her off saying, "Look Janet my mind needs a rest from all the Sledge troubles. Let's drop all that, at least until after we are home, then I promise I will try to discuss it with you."

After Jennie and Janet returned to Oklahoma, Jennie and I talked about how much of the truth about her family Janet should know. I thought she was mature enough to understand that even people who came from dysfunctional families could lead normal lives. Janet still had misgivings so I suggested that she serve up her history piecemeal to our daughter to observe how it affected her.

Working for Harry was no longer very challenging since Harry had stop expanding his business. This had given me more time to write; I wrote a memory piece called, *My Mother's Kitchen*, that had been accepted for publication and I was working on some revisions they had requested while I was at work.

Though it seemed premature to me Janet was already studying different colleges, she wanted one that fit her idea of psychology. When I discussed this with Jennie she told me that things were different now than they where twenty-five years or so ago when I went to college. Though I had spent years in amazement while watching my younger sister Nellie deal with her perceptive abilities, it still was hard for me to fathom what it must be like to live with a mind like she and Janet seemed to possess.

Josh's talent seemed to be in his drawings, some of which were very artistic. Some of his teachers had suggested he should look into the graphic arts field but Josh showed little interest in doing it.

During the school spring break, we all went to Sterling; I was going to have to come back after a long weekend but Jennie and the children planned to stay longer. What a change in Jennie's mother, no longer was she the poor lost soul. She was surrounded by seed catalogs and happily planning her vegetable and flower gardens. Mother, too, was more content than I last had seen her for a long time.

When I talked to Jason about it, he said, "You know Caleb I worried about moving back here with Mother being a burden on Lea.

Lea is so happy living on a farm with Mother and having Jean has made it better for us. Now Mother has a companion who is more her age to talk with and she is proud that we have been able to help Jean find some happiness. She was really upset about how Jean lived before; I used to try to tell her that there wasn't anything we could do about it. I guess that as bad as what happened is, some good came of it.

"Since you are going to be leaving soon, I'm going to let you in on a secret,

Caleb. Lea is pregnant. We didn't expect this but she is happy about it. I might be a little old to start a family but Lea is quite a few years younger then I am and very excited about it. She says it will be wonderful bringing a child up on this farm and we have two built in baby sitters."

I patted Jason on the back saying, "Age is not as important as you might think Jason, you'll be a great father. I agree with Lea, raising a child here can be great. I often wonder how my life would have been if I had stayed in Sterling. When are you going to tell the family?"

"Sometime soon, Caleb. Don't spoil it for Lea she has something planned. I told you because you might be gone before it happens." Jason said as he was leaving.

Jennie had once mentioned about Jason and Lea not having children and wondered if maybe they didn't want to because of their race difference.

The next few days Janet and I spent the mornings hiking mostly on Mount Fay. Josh wasn't too interested in going with us, he spent his time bringing life to Jean and Lea's garden plans by painting in the flowers and vegetables. Mother was ecstatic when she saw his paintings. She had always hoped Francis would amount to something in that field but he had given it up at an early age.

I hadn't seen so much buzz and happiness at the farm in a long time and it was infectious. I hated to think about leaving and was thinking about calling Eunice and asking if she could get my job covered for another week when I received a call from her.

She said, "Caleb, I hate to spoil your vacation time but could you come back tomorrow? Harry had an accident on his Indian and though his condition isn't critical, he thinks you have to get back here to help Shaq run the business. Probably Shaq would be all right without you for a few days but I don't want to upset Harry anymore than he is."

"Don't worry, Eunice. I'll get back on the first flight I can find, you tell Harry I'm on my way." I answered sadly hanging up.

It was three days before I could get a flight back to Oklahoma. Maybe it was at Jason's urging, but Lea announced that she was preparing a special meal the night before I left and no one was to enter the kitchen without her permission.

That night we had a fish and rice dinner that thrilled everyone and even though I had never liked rice, I enjoyed that meal. After everything had been cleaned up, Lea invited everyone into the parlor for a special announcement.

After everyone was seated, Lea said, "Jason and I have discovered something exciting we want your permission to add to the farm."

Mother said, "Now Jason, I still don't think we want a cow to have to care for."

Jason started laughing, Lea shushed him saying, "Definitely not a cow Mother Carney, something much smaller then that, though it might require more care then a cow at first. I'm pregnant and I'm praying this will be a welcome and joyous addition to this farm and family"

If Lea had any doubts about this being accepted, they were soon dispelled. Everybody was cheering as Mother, Jennie, and Janet rushed to give her a hug while Jean clapped her hands with the biggest smile ever on her face.

Later Jason told me he didn't know if this was some kind of a tradition or just Lea's way of wanting to announce the pregnancy.

As I was talking to Janet she said, "Boy am I glad it was being pregnant I sensed. I knew that she and Jason were hiding something from us every since we first got here. I was beginning to think that they might be breaking up. That would have been so bad for the family."

Early the next morning Jason took me to the airport, when I landed in Lotus, Eunice was there to pick me up and we stopped at the hospital to see Harry.

He said, "Sorry to have to call you back Caleb, but when I talked to Shaq he seemed nervous about taking over without you around. I'll be going home in a couple of days but I guess it will be a while before I do much traveling around. My leg is broke and I lost a lot of skin but the doc says as long as I don't get an infection I'll be good as new in a couple of months. I wish I could say the same for my old Indian, from the pictures Eunice showed me; it's in pretty bad shape. When you have a chance do some research Look for parts for a 1940 Indian. I'm going to need a lot of them. I just have to save her, she has been a part of my life for a long, long time."

As we left the hospital Eunice said, "What do you think, Caleb, are there parts around for something as old as that Indian?"

"It's quite possible Eunice, I never got into it much but I know Harry said there were clubs all over the world that do nothing but restore Indians, so I am sure in time we can get what his bike needs. I want to help him too. I never became a bike man, but I'll all ways remember the thrill of riding around Sterling on that old Indian. Remember, how every boy in town was my friend after Harry and his Indian showed up?"

Eunice said, "That seems so long ago, Caleb, and so much has happened in our lives since then but yes I remember the thrills Harry created when he first came to Sterling."

The next day at work I met with Shaq. I asked him what he was worried about. He said it wasn't the job he was worried about it was Harry.

"Eunice called me and I arrived at the hospital just about the time they brought him in. He was sure a mess, blood all over the place but he was conscious and wanted me to promise him that I would buy the company from Eunice if he didn't make it, just like we had talked about. I have never discussed buying the business with him or anybody else, though twenty years ago I might have been interested. I am much too long in the tooth to take on something like that now. Not wanting to upset him I asked when you were going to be back, so I could discuss the finances. I guess that is why he had Eunice call you. What the hell should I do about it Caleb?"

"I'm not sure what to make of it Shaq, maybe the best thing would be to wait and see if he brings it up again. People say things sometimes when they are in shock that don't make any sense. I could talk to Eunice about it if you want me to." I answered

"I guess you're right, it would be best to let it rest a while Caleb. I'll get back to you if it comes up again." Shaq said as he drove off.

Jason had worked out travel arrangements so Jean could go see Arnie at prison and Jennie, her mother, and Janet went to visit him before they came back from Sterling. He told them that Don had been down to see him and had a tentative court date in twelve months. Everyone was upset about waiting that long when they got back except Arnie who said he didn't find the prison any harder then being in the service had been for him. Aaron who knew more about Don's plans then any of us sent word that everyone who had worked with him was very optimistic that his approach would be successful in freeing Arnie.

After Jennie and the children came back to Oklahoma, our house was a whirlwind of planning for Janet's graduation ceremonies and for a big party after at the house. Janet had won several local scholarship awards and had received great offers from at least two of the colleges she had applied too. I had read some of the articles she had submitted and was surprised that they had been so well received. Though they were certainly well written, I found the subject matter slightly on the weird side. I guess, like Jennie said, it's a whole different world now than back when I started college.

Harry had healed enough so he was able to come to the party and had been available since he came home from the hospital to help Shaq running the business.

Shaq was still concerned about Harry's talk of selling him the business so a couple of months after Harry was back, Shaq asked Harry about it.

At first Harry seemed confused then laughed and said. "I'm sorry Shag. It's true that Eunice and I had done some talking about someday selling the business and she did mention that it would be nice if someone like you bought it. I don't really remember much of anything about that day, I can't even remember why I was where I was, or where I was supposed to be going. I don't remember talking to you that day but Eunice said you seemed upset about running the business with Caleb gone, when she met you at the hospital. I have no immediate plans of selling but if you are interested, I would be willing to discuss it with you."

"Like I told Caleb, I'm too long in the tooth now to want to start running this business but when you're ready, I have some younger friends that would be very interested. They come from the old tribe and they would continue using the kind of men we hire. I think with them, Jackstone Steel would continue to build its legacy." Shaq answered earnestly

"That's it, that's it!" Harry answered. "That's exactly what Eunice was getting at when she said someone like you Shaq. Thank you for caring that much about Jackstone Steel. I most certainly will talk to you before looking for any other buyers when I'm ready to sell."

Summer seemed to fly by, Jennie and Janet had taken another trip to see Arnie. He was doing well and didn't seem unhappy about being in that prison. Janet had chosen Hamilton College over in Clinton, New York. Jennie and I had hoped for a college closer but we didn't force the issue. Eunice and Jennie decided to fly out there with her and spend some time in Clinton until Janet got settled in.

Jennie was hesitant to go at first because Josh would be starting school while she was gone. Josh convinced her by saying, "Mother, I'm going to be all right. Dad will be here. I'm not your little boy just starting my first day at school. I'm in high school you know. Maybe Janet thinks she doesn't need anybody but we don't know that. What we do know is I will be all right, so your duty is to go with Janet."

I thought, listening to Josh, how much he rationalized like my late brother who he was named after. How proud my brother Josh would have been of him, he had a bright future in many fields. He not only was good at painting and drawing, he got excellent marks in the mathematics. Watching Janet in her college search made him do a little research for himself. Though he had another year in high school he was leaning towards studies in the electrical field. He had explored taking arts courses but decided it could end up being a waste of time. I wondered when I heard that if maybe my ending up in accounting after studying journalism had influenced him.

After Jennie and Eunice had come back from settling Janet in at Clinton, life became mundane since Harry bid on very few jobs. Crunching numbers every day became so routine that I could spend time writing during work. I had many more rejections then acceptances but I tried not to let it get to me, besides if I didn't write, I would go crazy sitting around the office.

There was good news from Arnie, Don had worked out a deal with the prosecutor's office for him to plead guilty to involuntary manslaughter. Don couldn't get the deal for time served, so they finally settled on four years including time served. Arnie said he was happy with that and with good behavior, he expected to be out sooner.

Josh graduated from high school and had decided on a two-year technical college not far from Sterling. Though it was over an hour drive from Sterling, he decided to stay at the farm. Janet had returned for her third year at Hamilton and Jennie and I were alone facing the empty nest syndrome.

That winter Harry received an offer for his company from the group that Shaq had talked about. Harry hadn't been the same since his accident and Eunice encouraged him to look seriously at the offer. Months went by as they dickered every aspect of the sale. According to Shaq this was normal procedure for that group. The group was made up of men who either had Indian blood or were concerned about Indian matters and bought up companies that employed workers from the tribes.

When most everything had been worked, out Harry came to see me saying, "Caleb, there is one big sticking point and it concerns you. They have their own accounting department and though they want you to stay on for a few months if I sell, they really don't see a future for you in their plans. I told them I wouldn't sell unless you were taking care of. They have come back with an offer of buying you out based on the years you have worked here, with part of the cost coming out of the sale. I told them you would have to agree to that before I would consider my end."

Though I had heard some rumors about this, it still was a surprise to hear it laid out like that. Eunice had been telling me that Harry was under a lot of stress, partly about selling and partly because the effect a sale would have on the rest of his help and me.

"Thanks Harry," I told him. "I know you are concerned about my job but if they have an offer, tell them I'm open to hearing what it is. This might even be a good thing for me. To tell the truth, bean counting every day has become kind of boring. For the last few years I have been getting back into writing like Aaron told me I should. I always planned to write when I retired; of course in my plans it was going to be the great American Novel. I suppose with two kids in college I'll have to plan something less of a gamble then that, but I probably can get a job writing somewhere and still work on it."

The following week I received a written proposal of what they proposed to do. The buyout itself was lower then I expected. After studying it and discussing it with Jennie, we made some changes. I asked for the same pay scale for the three months they were asking me to stay and asked for a specific increase in their buyout offer. Jennie brought up the insurance issue, which they hadn't mentioned. So we made carrying our insurance one of our requirements. A week or so later they wrote back with their comments. They had adjusted down my figure for the buyout by less then half of what I had added. The insurance was a definite no, though they said they were studying to see if they could carry me on their payroll for a year so I would be covered. After we had discussed all this with Harry and Eunice and hearing it would be at least six or eight months before a sale was concluded we decided to agree to their terms if their insurance plan was possible.

Chapter 9

It took over a year for the company to raise the finances and settle all the paper work needed to purchase Harry's company. I worked three months beyond that helping them incorporate Harry's books into theirs.

Actually it wasn't much work for me, all I was really needed for was to answer questions about differences that came up during the transfer.

After my three months were up, Jennie and I decided to take a vacation. We flew back to New York and rented a car to drive us to our old haunts.

The Jolene's had both passed on and their son George was running the farm. Though he didn't recognize us at first he seemed genuinely glad that we stopped and invited us to stay for dinner. At the dinner table he told story after story about Jennie's stay there and how jealous he and the boys around had been of Jennie's commitment to me.

We stayed at the farm that night and went to visit the newspaper office where I had worked the next day. There wasn't anyone left working there from the old days and the paper had changed completely. It was now a monthly paper that concerned itself with just the local doings of the surrounding towns.

As we left Jennie said, "It looks like we made the right move in leaving here Caleb, progress seems to have missed this part of the country. Let's drive down to Tupper Lake and see if we are lucky enough to get our old cabin. Maybe it stayed the same, too. Wouldn't it be wonderful to spend a few days there and do the things we used to do there?"

"That's a good idea Jennie. I'm not sure that we can recreate the same excitement of the first time we were there but I'm sure game to try." I answered laughing.

At the lake, most of the cabins that had been close to the lake had been torn down and a more modern motel type building had replaced them. The cabins back from the lake were still standing, including the one we had been in but looked like they weren't being used much.

The first person we talked to was adamant that we couldn't rent it but after hearing why we wanted it, the owner said, "Look, give me a couple of hours and I'll get someone up there to make it ready and clean it up. Far be it for me to deny a dream as romantic as yours."

Happy at our stroke of luck, we went down by the lake to a restaurant we used to go to when we were here before. We were happy to find that the dinner boat trips were still in operation, though it was a different boat now.

After spending a couple of hours by the lake we went back to check on the cabin. There was a young couple just leaving.

"We gave everything a good cleaning even changed the mattress and bedding," they said smiling from ear to ear.

Inside, everything looked very much as we had remembered it with the exception that it was cleaner and there was a bottle of wine and a candle on a little table by the bed.

Jennie said, "Well Caleb, just how much did you tell them anyway?"

"I only said, we were here on our honeymoon over thirty years ago and it had always been our dream to someday return to the same cabin. I love their imagination though," I answered laughing

We spent the afternoon settling in at the cabin and took the boat trip for our dinner meal. Cruising around the lake brought back many pleasant memories.

Jennie said, "Caleb, it's so hard to believe that so many years have passed. It seemed only yesterday we were here as young lovers."

Holding her tightly, I laughed saying, "Well Jennie, we might not be young, but we are still lovers aren't we?"

That night at the cabin with our wine and lit candle we made wild passionate love until we were exhausted, though the exhausting came much sooner than the last time we were here. We cuddled in each other's arms reminiscing about our life, our children, our dreams accomplished and unaccomplished until we fell asleep.

I awoke to the smell of the coffee, a cup of which Jennie handed me while admonishing me with, "Do you plan to spend all your time in bed while we are here?"

"Well I thought that was what a honeymoon was for," I answered sipping my coffee.

"I have been thinking Caleb, wouldn't be fun to drive up to Inchoate and have lunch at the restaurant where we met Lorraine. After hearing her story I have often wondered what became of her. You remember her don't you?" Jennie asked smiling.

'How could I forget the girl who helped you trap me into marrying you, Jennie?" I said with a laugh. "Seriously though, that's a wonderful idea, wondering what ever happened to her has often crossed my mind."

We arrived in Inchoate shortly after noon only to find that there was a second hand store where the restaurant used to be. Nobody at the store had any information as to how long it had been closed, they only knew they had been there over ten years.

Later at a diner in town we asked if anyone knew any history about that restaurant. One of the older waitresses named Norma said it had quite a history but she wouldn't have time to go into it while at work. We made arrangements to meet her later that evening; she suggested a restaurant on the outskirts of Inchoate.

At seven that evening, Norma met us there saying, "I've had time to think since we met and I'd bet you are one of Lorraine's pairings, from some thirty years or so ago right? I wish Lorraine were here, she often wondered how her pairings made out. As far as I know she never had a chance to meet any of them again."

"That's exactly why we were inquiring about the restaurant, Norma," Jennie said, "We are back in this area reliving some of the magic it has held for us then, and have often wondered what had happened to Lorraine."

"Well what happened is kind of prophetic. There was this young woman from Iowa who was up this way on some kind of a hush, hush assignment, who ate regularly at the restaurant. One night a young feller joined her. At first she seemed pleased and surprised but as the night wore on she became angrier and angrier. Finally she jumped up dumping the table on him and slapped him real hard and rushed out. Lorraine went over to see if she could help, the young man was covered with food and had tears running down his face. Sensing he was distressed setting there in public, she escorted him out back and helped clean him up. It took him a long time to pull himself together and Lorraine soothed him as much as she could. Finally he paid his bill and asked if he could go out the back. The cooks remarked, 'Bet we won't be seeing him again.'"

"Much to Loraine's surprise, a couple of nights later he came in again, telling Lorraine after all she had done for him he couldn't leave without explaining about what happened. He told her a classic story of childhood sweet hearts and the heartbreak when one of them gets a big break working for an elite company with people way beyond their normal living status. He had followed her up here with a ring and the hope that he could impress her enough to keep her."

"Lorraine never saw the woman again but Joshua, that was his name, stayed for about a week. About six months later he was back again for a week and he and Lorraine seemed an item. He showed up about every six months or so for the next couple of years. The last time he was here Lorraine made arrangements with her friend, the one who married you and went back to Iowa with him. Later, she sent an open letter to the restaurant that was posted. It said that although she missed her old friends, she was very happy out there and she wanted us to be happy for her."

"Norma, thank you, your story about Lorraine has made our trip so much better. We knew her story about losing her first love in the war and worried she would let the hurt keep her from finding happiness, so now like her letter asks, we can be happy for her." Jennie said, wiping a tear from her eye.

We spent the next couple of weeks at the lake, lolling around in our cabin, taking drives around the area, trying out new restaurants for lunch and breakfast and having most of our dinners on the dinner boat cruise. We had planned to drive straight to Sterling from there but after a late start and a couple of sightseeing side trips, we decided to spend the night in Albany.

Leaving Albany early the next morning got us to Sterling well before noon. Jennie's mother was out in the garden.

Lea was in the kitchen changing the baby and she said, "Caleb, I'm glad you could make it. Your mother isn't doing too well and I can't convince her to see a doctor."

Jennie and I went into the living room where Mother was and we were taken back at how much she had aged since we were here last.

I went over and gave her a kiss and a little hug saying, "Mother, what's this I hear about you're not feeling well?"

"I'm alright, Caleb," Mother answered, "just growing old. I guess there isn't anything a doctor can do about that. Lea keeps insisting I should go but I don't think I have anything we have to worry about. I tell you what, just so it will relieve your mind while you're here, if I'm not any better tomorrow I'll let you call the doctor, fair enough?"

Jennie went out and joined Lea with the baby. Jason Junior was near a year old now and Jennie couldn't wait to get her hands on him. I stayed and talked to mother. I told her all about how the sale of Harry's business and our trip back to New York.

A couple of times I sensed she was dozing off. When I asked her if she wanted me to leave she said, "No Caleb, stay. I want to talk to you about the farm. I wondered, since you don't have a job now, if you would be coming back here. I think it is time for the family to decide what should be done with the property after I'm gone. Now none of that maundering language, we have to face the fact that I'm getting to the age where it makes sense to do some planning."

"Okay, Mother, okay. I haven't given it any deep thought, but if I was to ever come back to Sterling, what I would want is that piece of land where we burned out. But I don't foresee us ever coming back here to live. Jennie's memories here aren't the kind that makes her want to return to Sterling and I have sort of grown out of any strong desire to return. I think that because Lea has such a love for the farm and Jason seems happy here, and if the other children don't object, Jason is the one who should inherit it."

"Well," answered Mother, "This might be easier than I thought. I have talked to everyone except Homer and Nellie and they all believe Jason should keep it. That takes a lot off my mind, Caleb. Now you go play with Jason Junior and Jennie. I guess I will nap a little."

"What do you think, Caleb?" Lea asked, "Don't you think she should go in for a check up?"

"I really don't know Lea," I answered, "She seems rational enough, though I agree she doesn't look well; let's wait until tomorrow. She said if she doesn't feel better then she will consider going in."

I spent the rest of the day wandering the farm; there had been some major changes in the garden. Jennie's mother had planted things we never did. Besides what we usually planted she had turnips and parsley, lettuce, parsnips and there was evidence of an early pea patch. She had pruned and rejuvenated the black berry patch so that it was in rows and not in the bramble we had always fought when we picked in it.

That night at the table, when I congratulated them on the garden, Lea said, "Don't congratulate us Caleb. Jean is the gardener here. She doesn't even allow us to pick stuff for fear we will do some harm. After Jason gets the garden ready in the spring, she's the boss from then on. We even had to fight to be allowed to help doing the canning. Finally the garden started producing so much she had to let us help."

"I hope you all understand what the garden means to me. Before I married, my family always had a big garden. Where we lived after I got married there was little room for a garden, besides my husband always said it was stupid to do all that work when you could get it from free from most of the neighbors. This garden not only carries me back to my youth, its that I am able give these plants the loving care I was denied giving my children. I find a blissful serenity in my garden watching God's magic as the seeds I plant grow. I thank God every day that he has created such wonderful people as the Carneys and for me being able to be on their farm," Jean declared breathlessly.

Lea said, "Jean, I believe everyone here would agree that even though your name isn't Carney, you are as much a part of the family as any of us are. One thing is for certain, your garden expertise has made you such an important part of the farm, and I don't know what we would do without you. You not only supply us with an abundance of vegetables we even sold enough at the stand to pay for the cost of the seed and fertilizer and then some."

After supper mother excused herself and went to her room to rest. Jason and I sat in the parlor while the girls were in the kitchen doing the dishes. Jason Junior had fallen asleep on Jason's shoulder. I asked Jason how things were going for him.

He answered, "Really wonderful, most of my work keeps me close by and Lea, Mother, and Jean keep everything here running real smooth. Lea and Jean are happy running the farm and Junior is fitting right in. Also Josh stays with us when he isn't on one of his trips, seems that he's working with some others evaluating a bunch of hydro electric plants all over the country."

"But I am concerned about Mother. Her health seems to be failing fast. She has been talking about turning the farm over to Lea and me. Not that I would mind but I would want a clear understanding with the rest of the family first. I am financially able to compensate all of you a fair share of its market value."

"I'm not sure about everybody else in the family, but all I would be interested in is still being able to stay here a couple of times a year just like I do now." I answered.

"What the hell, Caleb?" Jason exploded, "What do you think? I wouldn't welcome my family here just because my name is on a deed."

"No, no, Jason. I was just saying you don't have to pay me anything," I answered hurriedly.

Just then the girls came in and Jennie said, "Don't tell me the Carney boys are arguing. I don't think I've ever heard that before."

"No Jennie. It was just a misinterpretation of what Caleb was saying. I guess Mother's condition has us on edge. Mother has been discussing signing the property over and we were discussing how best to do that. She is afraid that if it becomes an estate, there might be problems settling it with most of us being married and having children." Jason answered.

Jennie said, "There shouldn't be anything to discuss. Whatever Mother wants is the way it should be. I'm sure that as long as Caleb has a place he can land in Sterling, he'll be happy."

Jennie's mother Jean, who had always so quiet surprised us all by saying, "I believe that Helen will be with us for a long time. If she does decide to transfer the deed to the farm to one of you, I want it understood I go with it."

We all laughed and I said, "Remember Jean what Lea said, you are considered one of us now, besides, none of us could make the gardens produce the way you do. Whatever agreement we make you can rest assured you would always be here."

The next day Mother called us all in after breakfast saying, "Like I told Caleb, if I didn't feel better today then I would see a doctor. My one condition is that all of you here promise me if I go, you will start procedures to have the deed to the farm transferred to Jason and Lea. I want to hear you say it, then Lea can call the doctors office."

After we had all solemnly promised. Lea went into the other room and called the doctors, she must have made it sound urgent because she came back and said, "It's all set for two this afternoon. Caleb will you be able to go with us?"

"Certainly, Jennie and I can both go, Lea. Then you can stay with Junior, if that's what you want." I answered

"No, no Caleb," Jennie cut in, "I'll stay with Junior. Lea will be of much more help because she knows how your mother has been much better then I do. Besides I have been looking for a chance to have Junior to myself."

At the doctor's office, Lea went in with Mother for her examination. It seemed that they were taking a long time and when Lea and the doctor came out, I could tell by Lea's face the news wasn't good.

The doctor, realizing I was her son, said, "Your mother is a very sick woman. Without further tests that I can't do here, I'm not prepared to make a diagnosis. She will need to be hospitalized for a least a couple of days. Her body is not functioning properly and I need those tests to figure out why. She has agreed to that, but she made me promise there would be no operation or invasive procedures without her knowing ahead of time and having time to discuss it with her family. That will be okay because it'll be a couple of days before we have any idea what were dealing with."

Lea and I took mother to Oscine to the hospital and waited until the nurses had got her settled. I told Lea she could take the car and go back and later Jennie could come and get me.

Mother said, "No Caleb, the doctor ordered some tests right away and I will be busy and the nurse told me not to be upset that they would be giving me a mild sedative, so nothing would bother me. I probably will sleep the day away, so why don't you wait and come back tomorrow."

Not wanting to upset Mother further, I went home with Lea with every intention of coming right back. By the time we arrived back at the farm, it was almost time for Jason to be home and Jennie said I should wait for him.

When we finally were on our way Jason said, "Caleb, I have suspected for months now that Mother was sicker then she ever let on, she has been discussing signing over the property for over a year now."

"I don't think that is to relevant Jason, "I answered, "It seems like that would be a pretty normal thing at her age. I, for one, am glad she is able to let us know what she wants. I don't assume there would be a big problem if we had to settle the estate amongst us but it's so much better doing it now in a way that she is content with."

At the hospital Mother was awake but a little drowsy.

After she got done chastising us for coming back before morning she said, "I don't want you two boys getting morbid about this but I want you to remember that I am here because of a promise that you would get right to work on transferring the deeds to the farm."

Jason laughed saying, "I don't know about getting morbid Mother but Lea called me at work and insisted that I ask Tom to draw up the necessary papers. He said he would have a request for the information he would need tomorrow morning. Lea told me she had promised you she would push this for you if you were laid up. Caleb and I don't stand a chance with Lea, Jennie, and Jean taking your place keeping us in line."

"Life is funny," mother answered whimsically, "You know, after Dad was gone and every one of the children had moved on, I thought I was strong enough to carry on alone. Soon though, I was an older woman facing years of aging alone and lonely. Then Jason's Lea came back with him, followed by Jean Sledge and life began having meaning again. Then as if life wasn't serene enough, Lea gets pregnant and little Jason comes and adds to the delight."

"You know, raising all of you has been a joy and a struggle. Now I'm blessed in my later years with new joys but without the struggle. Tomorrow I am going to be having tests all morning. We can't expect answers right away so I don't need all of you to be running to the hospital. What I do need is a solemn promise that if I have a bad diagnosis, you won't allow them to use life support when the odds are against me recovering whole. Now I want you both to swear to that."

Jason and I both shouted, "We swear."

Just then they announced visiting hours were over.

Both of us were lost in thought most of the way back to Sterling.

Just before we arrived Jason said, "I have a bad feeling that Mother has been hiding something from us Caleb. Otherwise, why would she be so adamant that we swear to all these things?"

"That thought has crossed my mind Jason," I answered, "but I keep telling myself that it is probably normal for her age to be concerned about such things. I'm glad that Jennie and I are here to help you and Lea. I certainly don't have answers for all this but at least you don't have to make decisions on your own."

"What will we do if she gets bad and they want to use artificial procedures that will keep her alive on a machine?" Jason asked just as we pulled into the yard.

"I don't think we should get into that as a family right now Jason. But if the time comes, remember, she said 'if the odds were against her' and that gives us some leeway." I answered as we got out of the car.

The next few days the doctors kept telling us they needed more tests. After one morning visit, I decided to walk around town.

The library was the same, the Inn was a little more dilapidated but was still functioning much as it used to. I started to go to the milk barn, but remembering how different it was last time; I decided I preferred to keep it as it was in my memory.

I walked by the Coors' barn on my way to the mountain and, remembering my tryst there with Beverly, wondered where she was now. I climbed slowly up to the tower. The tower was fenced in now so I couldn't go up. I sat by the big rock at its base, allowing wave after wave of my mountain memories to flow through my mind.

There was comfort in my reminiscing. Looking back at the joy, the fear, and the consternation of my trails here, I saw how much they were like life everywhere. Walking back down the mountain I remembered the exhilaration of our youthful runs and made an attempt to imitate them. I hadn't run very far before I realized that instead of exhilaration I was probably getting primed for a heart attack and decided to leave the run, like the milk barn, to memory.

That night the doctor asked Jason to have as many of the family as possible come to the hospital. The next day we were escorted into a small room to wait for the doctors. When they came in, they apologized for taking so long to come up with a diagnosis.

Mother had an aneurysm that was close to her heart and a weakened immune system. Though there was an operation for an aneurysm of that type, they were very hard on the patient and they didn't believe Mother had better than a fifty chance of surviving that operation at her age and condition.

There was an eerie silence after the doctors spoke. Finally broken when Jason hoarsely asked. "What does having an aneurysm like that mean, is it a death sentence?"

"Not necessarily," one of the doctors answered, "People have been known to live many years with one, but your mother's is well extended and could rupture anytime. We really couldn't put a time on it because there isn't any way to gauge the strength of her veins, without endangering her further. We, of course, will operate if that is your decision. Our job is to present the test results to the patient and the family."

"My God," I burst out without thinking, "you haven't told her all this, have you?"

"No," he answered, "but we have had some very interesting talks with her and I think you all know, she should be told."

In my heart and mind I knew what he was saying was true but I was still having trouble accepting it myself.

So I said, "Maybe in a few days, after we have a chance to absorb this, we can divulge at least some of it to her."

Lea said, "I know it isn't my place to advise at a time like this, but I have spent more hours with your mother lately than anyone of you, and I want to say something. Your mother is a wonderfully strong woman and she would be devastated if she had to live the rest of her life knowing you were hiding things from her. Your sister Nellie and daughter Janet didn't come by their sixth sense by accident, it's in the genes. I believe that she should be in here with us now hearing it from the doctors just like we are."

Jason and I just stood there looking askance of each other when Jennie said, "She's right Caleb. Let's get her in here right now while the doctors are still here."

The doctors had her brought in and told her basically what they had told us.

Mother hardly showed any emotion as she said, "It's bad but to tell the truth, it's not as bad as I feared. Despite the fact that this was supposed to be kept from me, I have always been good at weeding out the truth from my children so it wasn't hard from what I heard and got out of the nurses to find out about the aneurysm. I do have some questions though, what will it be like for me if it breaks?"

"I believe, Mrs. Carney, that it will be peaceful," one of the doctors answered. "You will have massive blood loss and will experience a great tiredness with little, if any, pain."

"Well, that is a great relief," Mother exclaimed. "I had envisioned something like a terrible cancer and having to live my life out in pain and misery. I thank you all for being forthright with me and now I want you all to join me in seeing this as good news. Now get me back to the farm!"

Back at the farm we were surprised to find that Josh was back. Jennie, to his embarrassment, was all over him, hugging and kissing him. It reminded me that she hadn't seen him for several months. He seemed to rather enjoy spending his time at the farm when school wasn't in session. Jennie often complained how hard it was to get her men to leave Sterling.

After Josh broke free from his mother, he hugged his grandmother saying, "It's good to see you home Grandma. I heard from Jean that you were in the hospital and I was worried."

"You needn't worry Josh, just a little aging problem. The doctors gave me some medication and everything is going to be alright." Mother answered with a smile.

When we came home to Sterling we had planned to only stay about a week but with Mother's illness and with Josh back, we decided to stay at least another week.

Josh joined me in exploring some of my old haunts. At the Coors barn there was still enough of the old bullpen to explain to Josh how breeding was done way back when.

He said, "I bet most of the kids in town got their sex education sneaking up here and watching. I know I would sure have been interested."

I thought, *Funny, I wouldn't want my son to have seen or been involved in much of what I had during my youth here.* Realizing that my folks never really knew about much about what I did then, made me wonder what had he seen or done during his years of puberty.

As we left to climb the mountain, Josh started talking about all the hydro plants he had been visiting. He was very excited about the prospects of some of them. There were a number of plants that used to run paper mills and other factories that had been given up when it became cheaper to buy electricity. Many of these plants were no longer in operation but now with electric power so much more expensive, Jason was working with a group as part of a college course to evaluate the feasibility of rejuvenating some of the best ones. Listening to Josh I felt good that he had found something he was so interested in that had the potential of being a good business to be involved in.

That night at the table, Mother said, "I only want to have to say this once, so all of you listen close. I know there have been discussions about what is the right thing to do about my aneurysm. There is no room for discussion. The doctors have given me medication that has made me feel much better and that's all that is going to be done. No operation and no treating me like an invalid. My medication is helping rebuild my immune system and every day I feel stronger. My aneurysm doesn't make me sick and if it burst then God has willed it and it was my time. This is the last word on any of this but I will promise you if I start going downhill again, I won't wait so long before I see a doctor. "

I think we were all glad that Mother had taken the decision out of our hands and we all worked hard to keep things as normal as possible.

Tom had drawn up the papers to transfer the farm to Jason. Those of us there readily signed it and Jason, who had been in touch with the rest of the family, sent copies around to all the family.

By the end of the week Josh was back in college and even though he came home nights, he was seldom seen as he spent his time pounding the books, as he called it.

That Sunday afternoon Jason dropped Jennie and me off at the airport and we were on our way back to Oklahoma.

Chapter 10

Jennie and I discussed Josh and Janet on the flight back to Oklahoma. Though we were both happy about Josh's enthusiasm with his hydro projects, Jennie was worried that we wouldn't see him at all if he went way up North to the sites he just returned from to work. I was pleased to see him so happy about what might become his life's work. Though working for Harry had been a good move financially for us, I had never looked at the job with the joy Josh was showing for his prospects; though I might have if my work had been in journalism. Josh had two more years of college to go and who knows what his plans might be then.

Janet, who was graduating this year, had already spent one semester over seas and was planning on trying to get employment with a company that would allow her to go back. I wondered if it had something to do with her sixth sense thing; my sister Nellie, who she was like, spends more time overseas then she does in the States.

When we arrived at the house, there was a pile of mail that Eunice had been picking up for us, on the kitchen table. Most were bills, magazines, advertisements and a letter from the company that had bought Harry's business asking if I could give them a few more days.

As I was sorting through them I almost threw away another letter addressed to me from Ace Advertisements. The name somehow rang a bell so I threw it into the pile to be checked later. After we had checked out the property making sure everything was functioning properly, we went the local restaurant for dinner before going food shopping to re-supply the house.

Later that night as I was taking care of the mail, I opened the letter from Ace and found it was an employment application form. As I read the cover letter I recalled why I had recognized the name. Ace used to have contests that promised great rewards if you wrote some snappy prose that they could use in their add campaigns. Years ago on a lark, I had entered in several of them. Their letter explained that they were looking for an in house writer and had sent out application forms to addresses of all writers who had entered any of their contests. Thinking that wasn't anything I would be interested in I put the letter aside.

The next couple of weeks I spent searching for some jobs that required my journalism skills. I didn't have many interviews before I realized my age and lack of work record in that area became a definite determent to being hired.

I applied to the paper where I had worked with Jake right after I graduated from college, and they were willing to give me work at my old job but that wasn't writing.

Jake had been gone for many years, he had been killed in a plane crash and nobody who I talked to even remembered him. I left there thinking how sad it was that even with all Jake's enthusiasm for life and his job, he had hardly left a mark.

For almost three months I checked out every avenue available to me without finding anything that I wanted. I did work a few days back at my old office helping them co-ordinate some of Harry's older projects with theirs.

One evening, when I was feeling especially frustrated after a job interview Jennie said. "Caleb, I ran across that letter from Ace today, have you tried there yet?"

"No Jennie, I didn't give it a thought. It didn't sound like it would be anything I would like." I answered, "Besides it has been over three months and they must have filled that job right away."

Jennie was insistent, so the next day I went to the Ace building in Lotus.

The receptionist said, "You know as a matter of fact they haven't filled that job. I'll see if I can locate Ernie, he would be the one to talk to."

About fifteen minutes later the receptionist showed me into a small office that contained a big man with a booming voice, after introductions he said, "I'm sorry we kept you waiting, it took a few minutes to find the stuff you sent us years ago. Tell me about yourself and why you want this job."

I told him my sad story, how it had been so hard getting a start in journalism when I graduated from college because of all the G.I's. that graduated at the same time who had so much more worldly experience than I did. How I had joined a family business and worked as their accountant until it was sold and now was attempting to get back into writing.

He laughed saying, "I'm not sure that what we require would be the kind of writing your looking for but seeing what you sent us before makes me interested in talking to you about it. I know you probably wondered why we haven't filled the job yet. The truth is, we have filled it twice but they didn't stay. They didn't stay because this job requires a thick skin and it gets repetitious sometimes just finding the right word to satisfy our customers. Basically this is what the position requires: you sit in on our design meetings and using the customers and our designer's suggestions you write a prose that will stick in everyone's mind. What this takes is someone who can write hundreds of different versions to be picked from. Sometimes our customers and sometimes our employees get real sarcastic about some of the writing and that's why the last two people quit. What do you think Caleb, is this anything you'd want to try?"

"You know," I answered much to my surprise, "It is not the kind of writing I have been thinking of but I do find it somehow intriguing."

"I tell you what, we are meeting right away. Why don't you join us and see what you think then?" Ernie answered as he got up leading me to their meeting room.

There were about ten people including the receptionist in the room, all talking at once when we walked in. Ernie quieted them and introduced me around, saying. "This is Caleb Carney, he just stopped by to inquire about the writing job. Now try to be polite and not scare him off. Okay Gene, go on with the presentation."

Gene produced a colorful drawing that he placed on an easel at the head of the table. It was of some food but I wasn't sure what kind it was. He went on to describe how he had enhanced the colors a little so when it is photographed it will look like the real thing. There was a big discussion on what should be placed around it to make it stand out more. There was a tremendous give and take about what music should be played with it.

Ernie said, "Caleb, this is a new health food product and we are designing a television add for it. Your job would be to come up with a slogan that would stick in everyone's mind that hears it. You can imagine it as being spoken or flashed across the screen. That decision will be made after everything else is done."

The crew went back to its shouting out ideas. Since there were paper and pen at my seat, I started writing whatever came into my head as I listened to them.

Can't be beat, good to eat
A treat for your eyes and your palate
Pretty as a picture, healthy as a food
A special treat, that's the right food to eat
A special treat, that's healthy to eat
A very special treat, that's good and healthy to eat
Not a healthy food that taste like dust
But one with a taste that makes you lust.

Then a heated discussion started between Gene and Lonny. Lonny thought the picture should have a sparkling effect around it. Gene thought that would take your eyes away from the product.

Ernie came up behind me and said. "What do you think, could you survive these meetings?"

Before I could answer, Ernie shouted, "Hold it Boys, let me read you something."

Grabbing my paper, he read of what I had written. Everyone became quiet for a full minute, and then the shouting began again, only this time they were arguing over which one of the things I wrote would be appropriate.

Ernie said, "Caleb, just say yes and the job is yours."

"I don't know, Ernie," I answered "this could be fun but I don't know what you're offering and I don't understand what's so important about my doodles."

Ernie said, "Come back to my office and I'll work up an offer for you."

As we left the room, somebody shouted. "Make it a good one Ernie, we need to keep him."

Back at Ernie's office, he again studied my application saying, "I'm not sure we can afford the pay scale your asking for but I'm willing to offer you eighty percent of it with the promise that if your work increases our productivity I'll meet that price in six months. Our benefits are pretty standard but I'll give you a copy to take with you and expect an answer right away, is that satisfactory?"

Intrigued as I was about the job, I knew I needed to think on it before agreeing to work here.

So I said, "This is such a new concept for me. I'll need a little time to digest it all before saying yes or no, but I will inform you in a couple of days."

As I was leaving his office, Ernie said, "One thing, Caleb, win, lose or draw, would you be willing to sign over what you wrote today if we use any of it?"

"Sure Ernie," I said laughing as I left, "If you can use my doodles then I will sign them over."

Back at home I told Jennie about my strange interview experience.

She laughed, asking, "Are you seriously considering working there? I think it wouldn't hurt to give it a try seeing how it's the first time I have seen you even remotely excited about a job prospect."

"It's funny Jennie, part of me says that isn't writing, yet another part of me felt at ease in that meeting writing down whatever popped into my head. I have been thinking I should give it a try. If it doesn't pan out, I certainly won't be the first or the last to walk out on that type of a job." I answered, pondering the quizzical look on Jennie's face.

"I was just thinking Caleb," Jennie said answering my ponder, "Very soon we aren't going to have any insurance coverage and we have to take that into consideration at least until the children are both out of college. I looked over the benefit package you brought home and their insurance plan is adequate and in their good years they are generous with bonuses. I know their pay offer is somewhat lower than you were getting but I think you should consider taking the job, at least until something better comes up."

The next day I called Ernie with the news and he said, "Good. Now consider yourself hired and start expanding on what you wrote at the meeting and be here tomorrow by nine."

After I hung up, it dawned on me that I didn't have a copy of what I had written and the job immediately grew more intimidating. After telling Jennie what was said, I started a list trying to recreate the thoughts I had at the meeting.

Treat, eat, palate, plate, mate, sate, craving, leaven,
Buy our—to try a treat that's healthful to eat
Craving a treat that is healthful to eat??? Try our—
Satisfy your craving with the treat that is healthful to eat.
Slake your desire with the healthful treat
With a taste that can't be beat.
Slake your desire with—a health food that doesn't taste like dust
But has a taste that creates a craving lust.

I filled two whole sheets with things like this and after reading them, I thought: *Man these are childish.* But I had to admit to myself it didn't seem that way as I was writing them.

The next day Ernie led me to a little hole in the wall office saying, "This isn't much of an office Caleb, but you will only use it to write when you need to escape the bedlam that we create sometimes. We have a new project going on in the meeting room, why don't you join them?"

Most of the people in the meeting room were the same ones as before with the exception of one man who was introduced to me as Lenny, our in house architect. I later found out Lenny was retired and only came in to help when his expertise could be useful in creating ads.

Today they were trying to create an ad to be used by a big construction company that built and designed office buildings and malls. Gene had created kind of a fade away drawing that showed several different types of buildings in a misty background. There were loud discussions on whether they should use a clearer drawing with the buildings more focused. As I sat listening to their discussions, I tried to write something that could be used. Using that drawing, I wrote:

Is there a building in your future or your dreams?
Let us—help your dreams come true and make your future brighter.
Let us—build your ideas and dreams into realism
Let us make your building ideas, into plans, your plans into structures and your dreams into practicality.

Lenny, who was walking around the room, stopped to look at what I was writing and said. "Great ideas Caleb. I heard you were a natural at this, just don't allow the madness here interfere with what you do."

They didn't have new ads all the time at Ace; sometimes we would spend months trying to parse my wordings to satisfy a company. We sometimes had six or eight ads at a time to work on, I liked it when we were busy because it kept me from thinking how far this job was from journalism. Time after time the crew chose something from what I wrote at the first meetings so I spent most of my time trying to augment those.

Time went fast now that I was back into the daily routine of going to work everyday. The job was great in many ways. I was allowed to take as much time off as I wished, as long as I was there for their meetings and kept copies of what I was writing with me to improve on.

With the coming of spring, Jennie planned a big graduation party for Janet. Jason, Lea, Josh and Mother flew up from Sterling. Though Mother had made the trip a couple of times over the years, we were surprised that she came. Janet was elated, she had always seemed to have some special connection with Mother. Shaq and some of Harry's old crew came and it was good to see them again, even though they picked on me about being some big time writer now. Jennie's sister Janet showed up but only stayed for a couple of hours before she had to catch a bus back, something about not being able to get the time off, so she could not stay.

It was great having Josh and Janet both home and watching them joining together to take time to visit with everyone there. Sometimes seeing them now as adults brought a little pang of guilt as I wondered if I had been father enough. Jason and the group from Sterling could only stay for a couple of days after the party because he needed to get back to work. Soon only our daughter Janet was with us and she had plans to go back to Clinton by the end of the week for an interview that might get her a job overseas.

A week after Janet had left, she called all excited. She had been accepted for the job overseas but would have to leave right away and wouldn't have time to come home. She said she would send us information on what she would need sent to her after she was settled. Though we were both happy she was able to do what she wanted, there was a sadness that she was leaving so soon.

Jennie and I had already been acclimated to the empty house syndrome and had adapted ways to fill our time. Jennie had been becoming involved with the local church and its volunteer groups and found that fulfilling.

I spent much of my free time working on the next great American novel, though the little of it that I had revealed to my family and friends hadn't produced much encouragement. I do believe that my struggle trying to write a novel help keeping me sharp at work because of all the word searches I did while writing.

Time went fast for Jennie and me. It only seemed like yesterday that we had Janet's graduation party before she was planning Josh's. Jennie had wanted to have the party at home like Janet's but Josh called saying that we should have a party at the farm because he was leaving two days after graduation for upstate New York, to work with a group revitalizing hydro electric plants there.

After Josh's party, it was almost two years before we got back to Sterling for an extended visit. Mother still seemed healthy and happy with the ways things were at the farm. It was only about two weeks after we had returned to Oklahoma from that visit that we received a call from Lea and Jason informing us that Mother's aneurysm had broken and she had died during the night.

Mother had prearranged her services so there weren't any decisions for the family to make; Jason asked us to help make sure everyone in the family was notified. We had phone numbers and addresses for everyone but we couldn't reach Nellie who was over in Africa with her husband.

Mother's instructions asked that she be buried within 3 days of her death.

Knowing that it would be impossible for her wildly scattered family to gather that soon and feeling she would agree this was the only thing we changed of her wishes.

After failing to contact Nellie, Jason asked at work if anyone knew what we could do. Donald Langley, the lawyer who had defended Arnie, knew someone in the U.N office who arranged a way to contact her and get her a flight home immediately.

We had been able to reach our Janet; but because she needed a week to get a replacement and more than that to get back, she decided she wouldn't try to return. The family was good with that and I knew Janet would rather remember her grandmother as she was the last time she saw her.

At the church services, several of the family spoke of Mother and what a wonderful mother she had been.

Lea with Jean standing by her side at Mother's casket spoke saying, "We have all heard today of what a wonderful mother Mrs. Carney was. I want to speak of what a wonderful person she was. I had been with my husband Jason for some time before I met his family. I felt that perhaps because I was Asian, I wouldn't be accepted but from the first day I met her and without a word being spoken I knew how wrong I was. I not only was accepted as family but when Jason and I move to the farm with her, I was made to feel an equal partner in every decision. When Mrs. Sledge, Jean, standing beside me had problems, Mother Carney was there to help. Not just with open arms but also with a compassionate understanding that made it possible for Jean to blossom in a new way of life. It was then I could see I hadn't been accepted because I was special, but because of who Mother Carney was. She was special in so many ways, the way she gave to her community, and the way she raised her children, her consideration for everyone who knew her. For those of us who are a part of or know any of the Carney family will know them as her legacy."

Lea and Jean took their seats, with tears streaming down their faces. The pastor continued the services using passages from the bible that Mother had directed, closing with Mother's favorite hymn *How Great Tho Art.*

At the cemetery, as Mother had requested, there was only the pastor and the immediate family. As we were standing by mother's grave, we said our silent sad goodbyes, as we had before to Josh and Dad. I thought: *where*

*have the years gone? It had been almost fifty years since we buried Josh
and now the family is slowly joining him.*

As the pastor finished his part of the service, Eunice stepped to the head
of the grave and opening a folder said, "Mother sent this to me years ago and
asked that I read it as her finally goodbye thoughts for all of us."

Please don't weep for me, for where I go is a far, far better place
If you must shed a tear let it be for a short time wasted lamenting my empty
place.
God has a special time for each of us to hear his beckoning call
And a place where we shall all meet again, in his hallowed hall

As we left the cemetery each silently carrying special private memories of
our mother and times we enjoyed throughout the years with a wonderful
mother who, even after death has asked us to let her go in peace to God.

One by one we filtered into the reception that the church had prepared
for us at the town hall, bravely trying to remember all these people from
Mother's life that had gathered to honor her.

Later at the farm we sat reminiscing in the dining room sometimes tearfully.

Nellie said, "I just had a horrible thought. Not a premonition mind you,
just a thought. This is the first time we have all have been together since Dad's
services and this could be the last."

Nellie's burst of thought left us all quiet and as I pondered it, I could see
why she had thought that. While Eunice, Hester, Emma, Jason and I had been
able to stay involved in what was happening at the farm in Sterling, this was
the first time we had seen Homer in years. Jason said it was quite a surprise
when he picked him up at the airport and he was wearing leg braces.

We knew Homer's marriage hadn't lasted and that though his company
was located way out West, he still travel a lot. Mother occasionally would
receive letters from him but she had never mentioned he had a leg problem.
When we questioned him he just shrugged it off as "It happens, it happens."

Francis, worked in the state of Washington and had married there and
made it his home. Though he stayed in touch, he hadn't been home for years.

Nellie spends more time overseas then she does in United States so it was
easy to see where her thoughts had come from.

There was something else though unspoken, I'm sure that the others felt. As I looked around the room, I wondered when we had all become so much older looking. Though there were mornings when I felt older getting the day started, I still didn't think of myself as being old. I suppose the others didn't either.

Everybody had arranged to be able to stay at least a week and it was nice getting reaqauinted as a family again. Lea was a gracious host, not only was she gracious but the way she kept the house and meals, was like Mother was still there. I couldn't shake Nellie's comment about this possibly being the last time we're all together. It's true that the disbursement of the Carneys as we each built our own families had built some walls. Still we always had home, hearth, and motherhood that tied us together before. Now I feel like we are losing that. I know that mother's memory and teachings will always be with each of us, but the closeness that we developed as children seemed a far away thing.

As Homer and I took a walk around the farm he said, "Caleb, it's been such a long time since I been here. You remember how I always talked about blowing the dust of Sterling off my heels? I have often wished I could have been as content as you with life here but the truth is I haven't found any place that was better. I still sometimes dream at night about our days working in the cow barn and wake up sad that I'm not really there. You, me, Janet, Jennie, John, and Arthur: who would of thought then that I could look back at those times as being some of the best times of my life? You know, Caleb, how I was always after you about the way you treated Jennie? One of the happiest days of my life was when I heard you two got married. I always felt she was the one for you even though I was half in love with her myself."

I slapped Homer on the back saying, "That was one thing you got right back then. Jennie has been my everything so long now that I often wonder why it took me so long to see it. You know Homer, I have been writing about us growing up here and someday after I retire maybe I will pull it altogether in a novel that makes sense out of it."

"Promise me, Caleb, that you will make sure that I get one of the first copies when you do. And Caleb, take the maybe out of your thinking. That's one thing that hasn't changed, your putting decisions off until you have all the answers. Nobody starts out with things perfect, they build and then improve on what they have built. Now that you have got me excited about your novel, I'm going to bug you until you get it done," Homer answered as we headed back to the house.

Lea had prepared a roast pork dinner that was so much like Mother's that it was like she was there cooking the meal. Hester, Homer, Emma, and Francis and their families were all leaving the next day and as good as the meal was, sad nostalgia invaded our conversations.

Josh, who had driven down from Northern New York, drove those who were leaving to the airport next morning.

After we had seen everyone off Nellie said, "Caleb, let's go hike up Mount Fay. I love how you became so attached to the mountain. Maybe now that I'm older, you'll help me understand that and be really honest with me.

We took the old truck that Jason had refurbished to use around the farm and drove to the mountain. Driving that truck and heading to the mountain really took me back to all that Sterling had meant to me.

Nellie and I walked slowly up the trails wandering in and off the main trails as I talked about my exploits there. How I had roved the mountain as a young child. How we had blue berried there as a family, how it was a place for me to escape and dream and about when Karl and I or Jake and I had spent nights up here camping out. I even told her about Karl and I seeing Bob and Kate and how Bob almost ended up in jail for rape.

I told her how I had spent two days up here after losing Josh and how the mountain had answered my crying out. I told her about coming here with Joan and how we always raced down the mountain. We climbed to the tower and set and had lunch; after climbing the tower I felt slightly dizzy and wondered how I could have thought that was so much fun back at the times we had talked about.

Nellie said, "What do you think Caleb, are you up to one of those exhilarating runs down the mountain like you and Joan did?"

"Not at my age, Nellie, and if I remember right, I was with you the last time I tried it, and I almost had a heart attack." I answered

As we walked down the mountain, Nellie said, "There was one thing that has always bothered me, Caleb. How about when you came to the mountain with Etta? I don't believe I ever saw such a dramatic change in any two people in my life, what happened?"

"I guess the best way to explain it, is to tell you that Etta and I had a history before she came here and it was an attraction that could never have lasted and it took a trip to my mountain for us to be able to work it out." I answered hoping Nellie wouldn't probe any further.

As we arrived at the foot of the mountain at the truck, Nellie said laughing, "I guess that is just about what I thought at the time, Caleb."

Jennie, Josh and Jean were just returning from Oscin. Josh had taken the women to see Arnie. After he got back from the airport, Arnie had been living there since he got out of jail.

Josh said, "I wish I had known you were going up the mountain, Dad, I would have like to do that before I left."

"You two can go tomorrow Josh. Your dad never tires of running around on Mount Fay, reliving all his Sterling escapades." Jennie said with a laugh.

"I think it would be fun if we all went, don't you, Caleb? It was fun going to all the places on the mountain like we used to do. How about it Jennie, are you up to it?" Nellie asked.

"You know, Nellie, that is the one place in Caleb's life that I have never invaded. At first, way back when we were younger, I was angry that I was never invited to go there with him. As we grew older together I came to see that Mount Fay was a part of him that would never belong to me or anyone else but the mountain. Sometimes it is important that we each have some sacred place or memory in our lives and I am glad that Caleb's is only his mountain." Jennie answered

After the three of us had spent an afternoon on the mountain, we gathered at the farm for our last night before the rest of us had to leave.

After supper Jason said, "Let's take a walk, Caleb."

As we walked around the farm, I asked, "Do you feel like Nellie? That this might be the last time we all get together, Jason?"

"It's been on my mind, Caleb," He answered as we wandered through the wooded area where we had cut wood so long ago. "That's one of the reasons that I asked you to come for a walk. I have a big decision to make in the next couple of weeks, one I haven't even discussed with Lea. My company wants me to take a job in their office in England; I wouldn't even consider it except it comes with a big raise and it would make money matters so much better when I retire. I know Lea would consent to going even though she would hate leaving the farm but there's Jean to consider also. It has been good living here but I have passed up some other good company offers to be here. It probably would be all right financially now when I retire but I would be more than comfortable if I took their offer. I know this is a load right after Mother's death, but I could use some advice."

"You're right about one thing, Jason, it is a load. Maybe you could consider renting the farm out for the time you're gone and if you're lucky it would be with someone who would let Jean stay. If that's impossible then we could move Jean up with us and we have enough land so she still could garden, though it would be a lot less than she has here. I don't think I should try to answer for you Jason. I think you and Lea have to make the final decision but I don't think the family is going to be upset about the farm as long as it stays in your name." I answered hoping I wasn't showing the shock I felt.

"Thanks Caleb, you know with Mother dying, I couldn't see any way I could entertain letting the farm go but if I rented it or found someone who we trusted to keep it up for those years. Maybe something could be worked out. I have a couple of weeks to let them know so in a couple of days after I have done some investigating about renting, I'll talk to Lea. You know Caleb, this is like the old days when Dad was sick and I would come to you when things went wrong. Even though times were hard for us, those were good days weren't they, Caleb?" Jason asked with a little laugh.

The next day Josh dropped us off at the airport on his way back to New York State. Jennie held him like it was their last goodbye. Nellie's plane left an hour before ours and she had said, "Please try to stay in touch Caleb, this time together leaves me with a scary apprehension that I can't explain."

As our plane was leaving the runway, I was overcome with this strong feeling of loss that was hard to shake off. Jason's talk about leaving the farm, Homer's declaration, Nellie's apprehension, was Mother's death really the disbanding of the Carney family?

Chapter 11

A few days after arriving back home in Oklahoma, we received a call from Jason. He had discussed his job relocation with Lea and even though she felt sad about leaving the farm, she understood the value of the move.

She also thought it would be good for young Jason to spend a few years of his schooling in England. They had talked to Jean about it and she had suggested that maybe Arnie could come and stay at the farm and help her keep it running. Jason wasn't going to have to move to England for at least six months and he thought maybe he could work something out with Arnie. Jennie suggested that she could come back and talk with her mother and Arnie if Jason thought it would help. He told her he would get back to her if it became necessary.

Though our home felt sort of empty at times, there was the comfort of Jennie and me being alone again. Jennie filled her free time working as a volunteer for the town and church, finding satisfaction in this lifestyle. My job at Ace kept me somewhat busy and I spent my free time trying to write my novel with words that would portray the remembered emotions of my youth.

My years on the job at Ace had toughened my skin so the slings and arrows in our meetings, sharp as they were sometimes, never became imbedded in my thought process or affected me outside of the meetings. I had the good luck of having come up with wording for several advertisements that seemed to have lasted. So whenever Gene, Lenny or some of the others got too sassy, I would gently remind them that my contributions to those ads were helping to pay their wages. Still, as much as we all bantered in those meetings, no one seemed to carry any animosity about it when we had left.

One night after I gave up the struggle of pursuing my novel, I joined Jennie on the couch.

She said, "I was just thinking Caleb, this is how it is supposed to be. A couple of old fogies only involved in what we feel like doing most of the time, or pursuing a dream like yours of writing."

Though I held certain satisfaction in how our lives had unfolded, my writing about my youth had created a desire to somehow to be able to relive some of the emotions. I remembered writing about those times.

Feeling these thoughts would be upsetting to Jennie, and that there was truth to the old adage you can't go back, I said, "I don't know about that 'old fogies' part Jennie, but there is a joy in all that we have accomplished. With our children well on their way of establishing lives of their own and us on a relative easy street, maybe we should consider whether we are going to be content spending the rest of our lives right here or not."

"I have given that some thought, Caleb," She answered, surprising me. "I wouldn't want to move from Lynwood, there are options around here that we could move to, but I don't desire them. We have spent many years in this house and know it well and though we don't need all this room, I believe that if we were to leave this for a smaller place, we would have regrets. I, for one, am too content here to temp that kind of fate. What I have thought was that it would be nice to have a fireplace on cool evenings or maybe one of those new wood stoves with a glass front "

Though it never had been an open thought or discussion, in the back of my mind I had always envisioned my last years being in Sterling. Realistically I knew, because of how Jennie felt about Sterling, that wasn't likely to ever happen. Still the remembrances that I used in my writings lately have rekindled my desire to return.

Still, I blanked out those thoughts, saying. "We probably could afford building a fireplace but I think your idea about a wood stove is more prudent. I'll ask Harry or Eunice if they know someone reliable who can evaluate our chimney to see if it is feasible to hook a wood stove to."

Later that night Jennie shook me awake, saying. "Caleb, Caleb, are you alright? Your covered with sweat and you have been thrashing around and screaming."

"Just a bad dream, Jennie" I answered as I got up and wiped myself dry and changed my pajamas. "Something about a panther I guess, go back to sleep. I'm alright."

I didn't want Jennie to know about my dream; first a black panther was chasing me off Mount Fay. Then I dreamed I was running out of Sterling naked with a crowd of people chasing me. I guess I was having a Freudian reaction to my realization about not going back to Sterling.

Though Jason had consulted with us regularly about his leaving, it was almost six months before he had an arrangement that seemed plausible. Arnie was willing to live and work at the farm but he didn't want to have the responsibility of managing it.

Jason had talked about the farm and our plans at work and Tom introduced him to Mr. and Mrs. Farr, a couple that were looking for a farm where they could experiment raising llamas and pigmy goats as a hobby. They didn't want to invest in a farm themselves until they were sure they would be as happy doing it, as they were in the planning stage.

After viewing the farm, they were content that it would work well for what they had planned. Having Jean stay was not a problem for them and they welcomed the idea of Arnie being there to help run things.

They had envisioned pasturing most of the farm and letting their animals have free range, but this upset Jean and her vegetable garden plans. Mr. Farr sat down with her and devised a plan were they would fence in her garden area with a fence that could be moved a percentage every year, to go along with her desire to have some new ground every year.

Jennie and I spent a week in Sterling with Jason's family just before they left. Though there was some sadness, they seemed excited about going to England, especially young Jason.

We got to meet the Farrs, as they were over several times straightening out the legal arraignments that Tom, Jason's lawyer friend thought was needed. I couldn't get a good make on them, as they were so excited about their plans for the farm. They mentioned that Jason had discussed the fact that from time to time some of the family might want to stay at the farm.

Mrs. Farr said that wouldn't be a problem because they were planning on making their bedroom on the first floor and that left four bedrooms upstairs for Jean, Arnie, and any company that came.

The night before we left to go back to Oklahoma, Jennie and I sat in the living room with Jason and Lea. As we sat there talking, just the four of us, I recalled Nellie's words after mothers funeral, "This might be the last time the Carney's are all together."

Though she said at the time she wasn't prophesizing, now that Jason, the last Carney was leaving the farm, the words sure seem prophetic. The next day, before we left, Jennie had a long talk with her mother and brother, advising them both that if it didn't work out for them, we would be available to help them make other plans. As we said our goodbyes before leaving for the airport it again occurred to me how much older everyone seemed to have grown.

Later on the plane I asked, "What do you think Jennie, is this arrangement going to work out for your family?"

"You know, Caleb, I'm less worried now than I was when I first heard about it. Arnie is happy to have something to do that doesn't require him to manage things and as long as mother can keep on gardening the way she wants to, she seems content. I talked to Mrs. Farr about her household duties and she said she and mother had discussed it and she was sure they both were going to be happy working together. I liked what I saw about Mrs. Farr, what was your take on her husband?" Jennie asked.

"I didn't get a good fix on him but had a feeling that he has a possessive nature that I would find a little irritating."

When we got back home, Eunice already had someone over to inspect the chimney and though the chimney was okay, he suggest we have a fireproof area built where we wanted the stove placed. Eunice came over the day we arrived with his recommendations.

After telling us about the chimney, she said, "Caleb, I'm having a problem with Harry. I'm afraid his memory is getting bad and I don't know what to do."

I had seen some of this happening the last few months when I talked to Harry but had just put it down to his age. So I said, "I know he was having some trouble remembering things Eunice, but there isn't much we can do about growing older."

"It's not just his memory, Caleb. He sometimes thinks he's back when he was much younger and goes get his Indian motorcycle out and says he guess he'll go for a ride. He even got it started once before I caught him and if I hadn't been there he would have taken off with it. You know it has been years since he has ridden. Though he was able to get the parts to fix his bike after the accident, he never rode much after that. I'm really worried when I leave him alone. Caleb, what shall I do?" she asked, almost to the state of tears.

We could take the bike away but I don't like the idea of doing that. I know, I'll talk to one of the bike mechanics. I'm sure there is some way we can disable the ignition that won't be noticeable to him. That way we can still leave the bike there for him. We are all growing older Eunice. I guess we will have to look after each other better now." I answered, thinking who would have ever thought that something like this could happen to Harry.

It took Jennie about six months before she could decide on a stove and how she wanted her hearth to look. When it was finished, it was very much like having a fireplace. There was a flagstone base under the stove and the wall by the stove had been built out and covered with realistic looking fake stone, topped by a real stone mantel. Jennie had surrounded this with a new couch and chairs and lamps for reading with and we spent every cool evening, settled there in blissful contentment.

About a year after Jason and his family left for England, Jennie and I went to Sterling to visit her mother and brother. We had stayed in touch with how they were doing by calling at least once a week. After one call Jennie began feeling that we had been a little negligent, so we made arrangements to go back.

I was ambivalent about going back this first time because there were no Carneys at the farm but my writing had caused a yearning to be able to go to the Sterling of my youth.

Arnie picked us up at the airport with Dad's old truck, every time I got to ride in that truck I silently thanked Jason for having it restored. It sure turned heads, especially when they saw Jennie who was dressed to the nines getting into it. Arnie was pretty quiet most of the way until we were almost at the farm.

Then he said, "You will have to be careful with Mother, Jennie, things are getting hard for her and she fights having to give up doing anything. So far Mrs. Farr has been good about it but Mr. Farr has made a few remarks that I didn't like. We tried to get her to cut back on her gardening but she sees that as failing and won't listen to us. So far I have been able to help enough so that her garden does all right but she complains about me working in it, claiming she doesn't need any help. Mr. Farr suggested that we cut down on how much we fence for her garden next spring; she hasn't spoken to him since she heard about it. I don't think he meant any harm, he just thought that doing that would help her. The Farr's have been good to us but Mother says it wasn't like before when she when she always felt like family. I have tried discussing other options we have with her but she won't even listen any of them. I think we can hold on here for another year or so but maybe we ought to start thinking about her care after that."

Jennie said, "There will always be room for both of you at our home, Arnie, no matter what happens."

"I know that, Jennie, but if I was you I wouldn't bring it up to Mother right now," Arnie answered

At the farm Mrs. Farr was there to greet us. Mr. Farr was out inspecting fence as one of their llamas had been found half way to town. I found it uncomfortable as we were being shown to our room. I suddenly felt like a stranger on the farm that had been my home all these years.

After Mrs. Farr left and we were unpacking I said, "I feel like a stranger here now Jennie. It is so weird to be treated like a mere visitor here."

"I knew you were going to find it different Caleb, but give it time, it's not like the Carneys have lost the farm. Someday Jason will come back. I'm just so glad that with the Farr's, Mother and Arnie been able stay here. By the way what was your take on all that Arnie had to say about Mother?" Jennie asked.

"Well, to tell the truth, I have always marveled at how well your mother has done with her years at the farm. She has kept a work schedule that would have been hard for some who are half her age. It's sad that age is starting to catch up with her but we should be thankful that she is still fighting to go on.

Arnie feels she has at least another year, let's pray for more and plan our options for the inevitable," I answered.

"Caleb, even though you're probably right, that sounds so cold." Jennie said sadly.

The time I had to spend with the Farrs was a living hell for me. All they talked about was their farm, their animals and all their plans for the changes they were going to make. I tried to tell myself that this was only temporary and some day there would only be Carneys here, but neither that nor Jennie's happiness for her family relieved my anxiety.

I used the pretext of my writing as the reason I spent so much time carousing around Sterling. I actually had planned on researching some of the places I was recalling to write about. Now I just made it a full time excuse for being away from the farm so much. It was very disappointing going back and finding things so different after all these years.

The town barn wasn't there anymore and the Muldons were all gone. The cow barn and milk house where we had worked were still there but they were only being used for storage. It seemed that after milk pasteurization became the law, that small country farms couldn't get enough for their milk in bulk shipments to make it viable to continue running dairy farms.

They had added a room to the center school and torn down the big shed that used to be next to it. The swings were still in the same place and as I sat in them musing about old times, I saw some children pointing at me and laughing. I supposed it did look funny to them that some old man was setting in the kid swings looking so sad.

I spent hours on Mount Fay wandering the paths of my youth, recalling old escapades with relish. Mount Fay was one thing that time hadn't changed much, though there was considerable slash left from recent logging operations. It reminded me of one of Josh's poems he called *The Metamorphous.*

The woodsmen have left a jagged swath
I pray they reasoned well
That society would put to aesthetic use
Those trees, which they have fell
Perhaps to build a wondrous home

That another heart or mind will see
As holding all the awesome beauty
That the trees they cut, once held for me

In town much had changed. There was no longer anyone running the store and though most of the houses were much the same, people who have names I did not recognize occupied many of them.

The library was much the same with the exception the glass case with memorabilia that had been stored there for years was gone and there were plans to add on to the building. The Inn was still running but it looked like it hadn't seen any serious maintenance in years.

After making the tour of the places of my youth I decided that their descriptions as I remembered them would better serve my writings. Still on the day before we left Sterling I couldn't resist taking the old truck and driving to the spot where George and I had caught all those fish. Even that was a disappointment, the old dams had given way and there were only a few shallow holes left where the brook ran through instead of the little ponds we had fished.

The next day on the plane, Jennie said, "I'm sorry, Caleb, that it was so hard on you going back this first time since Jason left. If you don't think it'll be better next time, I could go alone to see my family."

"Having the Farrs at the farm was hard, Jennie," I answered, "but I will always want to go back to Sterling, even if I have to stay someplace else."

Back in Lynwood there were urgent calls from Ace on our answering machine. I called the office and they asked if I could come right over.

Ernie said, "Boy are we glad you're back. We are competing for a contract with a general food provider and if we win it, our finances would be set for years. They control so many different kinds of food they could end up being, if not our only customer, at least our major customer. We have several ideas for using different products; some in groups, others by themselves. What we want you to do is work with Gene for wording on what has been done so far. Be prepared for many diverse and late meetings. We only have four months before our presentation so we are pushing the weeding process and hope to have at least four ideas formulated in a month so we can polish, polish, polish right up to the presentation."

The urgency at Ace and the feeling of being important in their process, kept me too busy to be lamenting about what had happened in Sterling. I was lucky because I was allowed to walk out of most meetings as soon as I had a grasp on what was being attempted. Sometimes taking my notes to my little office and sometimes at the end of the day just going home. The meetings were more intense than ever but I only had to make notes grabbing wording from my mind about what they were presenting and send my final attempts back to Gene.

One time when I was deep in thought at home trying to parse some wording, Jennie came over and gave me a little shove saying, "Caleb, you haven't heard a word I said. Aren't you interested that Josh called today?"

"I'm sorry, Jennie," I answered sheepishly, "I was trying to find a more meaningful way of using some words."

"You know, Caleb," Jennie answered, surprising me, "I find what you do intriguing and have often wondered if I would be any good at something like that."

Handing Jennie a few pages of my notes, I said, "No time like the present to find out."

Much to my surprise Jennie and I spent many evening pouring over my notes. Soon it became almost a ritual.

We had been doing it for a couple of weeks when Gene called me in to his office Saying, "Caleb, there seems to be a big change in the way you have been wording some of your efforts. I'm not complaining, Caleb, though some of your thoughts seem to be leaning away from where the project is going, they are certainly food for thought. What I am interested in is what has made the big change?"

"I'm glad you don't see it as something bad because I would hate to have to go home and tell my wife she couldn't be involved in my work any more," I answered laughing.

"That's it, that's it," Gene almost shouted. "That's what this project needs—more input from a woman's point of view. We're working on food advertisements and women do the most of the grocery shopping. This gives me an idea; we need more women in those meetings. I'll have everyone ask their wives, girlfriends, mothers, sisters or any women they know to come to one of our sessions. Let's make it a contest with a money prize, like we used to do with our contests years ago."

When I told Jennie what had happened she laughed and said, "Caleb can I go to at least one of those meetings?"

Jennie attended a couple of meetings but found them barbaric although she still enjoyed working at night with my wordings. For the next couple of months she spent many nights going over my notes. This new exploring of each other's minds brought a new closeness between and even rejuvenated our love life.

It was so good and brought back so many memories, that some mornings I would wake up surprised that I wasn't back in our honeymoon cottage by the lake in New York. The idea of having women help at Ace had paid off to the extent that Gene and Lonny had already picked four of the projects for us to polish for the presentation that was scheduled next month.

One night when I arrived home I could see Jennie was upset and she looked as if she had been crying. I held her close, while trying to still my own heart and thoughts that were racing with the fear of what could only be bad news.

"It's Mother, Caleb. Arnie just called and they have taken her to the hospital. When she didn't come in for the evening meal Arnie found her out by her garden paralyzed and unable to walk or talk. Arnie is getting in touch with our sister Janet and I have to go to Sterling to be with them. I know you are needed at Ace right now Caleb. I'll go alone and you can come later when I need you."

Jennie had already made arrangements for a flight that night and had called Arnie to give him the time to pick her up at the airport.

Things were coming to a head at Ace but when I explained to Gene what had happened he said. "Caleb, we are pretty sure what we are going to use in our presentations. Though it would be better if you were here if we decide to change any wording, as long we can still get in touch with you, go if Jennie calls for you. Also you should tell her that her involvement was a big boost for Ace and if we get the contract you can expect a big bonus."

Jennie called everyday. The doctors weren't sure just what had happened to her mother and suggested she be put on life support system until they run tests to determine the problem. Jennie didn't seem very hopeful. Her mother hadn't recognized any of them since she got there but still they went every day. Janet had been there but had to go back to straighten something out at her office and would come back as soon as there was any change.

About a week after Jennie left, she called to tell me the doctors had told them there was no hope. Her mother had suffered a massive stroke and was brain dead and wouldn't last more then a day off the machines. I told her I would come right down she said to wait until the funeral arrangements had been made. That way I wouldn't have to be away from work so long. Janet was on her way back and the three of them were going to the hospital tomorrow to be with their mother after they unhooked the machines. I called Gene and told him I was going to stay home the next day to be available if Jennie needed me.

The day dragged on until about two o'clock in the afternoon the phone rang, it was Janet she was sobbing so hard I couldn't understand her.

She kept saying, "They're gone, Caleb. They're all gone."

I broke in, "Janet, Janet I know about your mother. Where's Jennie, why didn't she call?" Janet sounded hysterical.

I heard a man's voice say *let me have the phone.* "This is Officer Parker. To whom am I speaking?"

"I'm Caleb Carney and the woman on the phone is my sister in law. What is going on, why hasn't my wife called?"

"Mister Carney, there has been a terrible accident. I'm not sure of all the particulars but this women was by the side of the road screaming, 'I have to call someone, I have to call someone.' so I helped her make this call."

"What kind of an accident?" I asked fear climbing into my mind as I recalled Janet's *They're all gone, Caleb.*

"A truck pulled out of a parking lot onto the highway right in front of a big loaded logging truck. The woman in it was killed instantly and the man is in the emergency room with little chance of surviving."

I dropped the phone as a piercing scream started from somewhere deep inside me and it felt like a horse had kicked me in the heart, my whole body became numb.

I could hear the voice on the phone saying, "Are you there, Mr. Carney, are you there?"

Finally the voice said, "I need to take this woman into the hospital, I'll try to get back to you."

I don't know how long I lie there in shock but finally came to enough to call Eunice saying, "Help me Eunice, help me, Jennie is dead."

Eunice came right over and after calling to arrange care for Harry, made arrangements for us to fly to Oscin. Since it would be some time before the flight, she called Josh to inform him and asked him to locate his sister.

While she was busy doing this my mind was in a complete fog of denial, *this wasn't happening it was just one of my nightmares.* There was no way to accept this; I couldn't allow my mind to accept that Jennie was gone, truly gone.

Life was becoming a surreal fog of black pain; with Eunice guiding my every movement, it was like managing a mirrored sequence of events in another world.

Josh arrived in Sterling the day after Eunice and I had.

We held each other weeping quietly, when he said. "Mother would want us to be strong, Dad, as hard as it is going to be we must remember that. While driving here I remembered your story, about how uncle Josh's ghost had come to you on the mountain telling you that life goes on and to let him go. I feel that she is with Josh now and would want us to heed the same message."

Words, words, words, I kept hearing them from so many people. Words supposed to be of comfort and caring to a man that had been making his living parsing words. Now I am hearing them from this grown man who used to be my little boy. I didn't need to hear those words; I needed to hear that they weren't needed, that what they were talking about never happened.

Eunice came over and said, "Josh, were you able to contact your sister Janet?"

"Yes, Aunt Eunice, we were lucky she was already in the states and should be here by tomorrow." I heard Josh answering with a sob.

"Come on you two," Eunice urged, "Jennie's sister Janet wants to talk to us about the services. Do you think you're up to it, Caleb?"

As Janet came over to hold me I thought, my God when did she grow so old?

Janet held me whispering, "I'm sorry, so sorry Caleb. After we had watched Mother draw her last breath, I should have understood Arnie was in no shape to drive. We talked in the parking lot but Jennie said they would be all right and to meet them at the Oscin restaurant. As I was going to my car, I saw the logging truck and screamed at Arnie to stop but I was too late. That old truck just shattered into a million pieces and the next thing I knew, I'm with some police man trying to talk to you on the phone."

I tried to tell Janet it was okay but I couldn't, the words just stuck in my throat because I didn't feel as if anything would ever be okay again.

Finally Eunice said, "I have been over this with Janet, Caleb, and she is planning on holding a small service for her mother and Arnie at the cemetery and wondered if you would want to hold Jennie's service there at the same time."

Jennie's one concession to Sterling as I vaguely remembered it was that she didn't care if we bought our cemetery plot there, because she had always felt dead in Sterling anyway. Josh suggested that we wait until his sister Janet came the next day before making any decisions.

So I said, "Eunice, why don't you, Josh, and Janet work it out with Jennie's sister Janet and I'll suggest any changes I may want after you four have decided. I think that'll be better than having you or my children let my foggy thoughts control what happens."

The next week was like the most bizarre version of hell imaginable. Josh and Janet both were reaching out to me with their need and I was unable to help and the feeble attempts I made were ineffective.

My family, with the exception of Francis, who was recovering from a heart operation, and Nellie who they were unable to contact, all came. Harry called and said the church at Lynwood wanted permission to hold a memorial service for Jennie's friends there. Knowing that Jennie and I had been gone from Sterling for so many years we wouldn't be well remembered here I allowed the services in Sterling to be conjoined with Jennie's brother and mother.

Although the burials were at different cemetery plots the sites were close enough together for the service to cover both of them. The whole ordeal was a blur for me, I just kept blacking out. Most of the time Jason and Homer were holding me up; I remained unconscious to most everything except the screaming no that reverberated through my mind.

Emma and Eunice combined to give what I was told was a beautiful eulogy; Emma spoke of Jennie's youth in Sterling and Eunice of her years in Lynwood. Mrs. Farr spoke about what a special person Mrs. Sledge was and how her dedication to her garden and the earth was almost like a religion with her. The parson followed this with the usual Bible quotations and promises that I wanted to believe, but my mind kept screaming how could a just God let Jennie die.

The church in Sterling had insisted that we at least allow them to put on a reception, we agreed as long as it was kept to family only. At the reception I set in black despair as the family buzzed around me with their words, words, words. Didn't they know my Jennie had just been lowered into a black hole in the earth? There weren't any words that could undo that.

I heard Homer telling Josh and Janet how I had been when their Uncle Josh had been killed and they had to give me time. I knew I should be comforting them but there I sat so bitter and angry that even my children were looking somewhere else for comfort.

Lea, Jason's wife came and quietly sat by me holding my hand, I'm not sure how long she sat there but as she was called to leave she said, "Caleb, anger and despair are destroying emotions. Jennie wouldn't want you to be destroyed. If you open up and let him, God will help you through this."

Josh and Janet had both arranged to have some time off from their jobs so after the reception we spent a few more days at the farm. It didn't take long for Mr. Farr's *mine, mine, mine,* to get to me, so we made plans to fly back to Lynbrook.

Josh insisted that we should spend some time on the mountain before we left, so we spent most of the last two days we were in Sterling on the Mount Fay. I think that he and Janet thought that maybe the answer to my despair was up there somewhere.

After hearing from Homer about the release I got from my pain after Josh's death, they hoped it could happen now for their mother. Even I held some little hope through my fog of reclaiming that experience again. Though the familiarity and the memories there were helpful, there was no lifting of the despair that permeated my body.

As we came down off from the mountain for what could possibly be my last time I thought. *This was Josh's mountain. Jennie never came here, so searching for an answer here was never going to work.*

171

Chapter 12

Josh and Janet both went back to Lynbrook with me hoping that the three of us could somehow reconcile to the fact that Jennie was no longer with us. For me being back in the home that was so much Jennie, only managed to make my mental state worse.

The next week, it was so bad I was oblivious to the world around me. The people at Ace called continuously; I refused all calls and finally Josh told them maybe it would help if one of them came over. Gene came over to tell me we had won the food contract and how lucky they were to have me, because I was responsible in a large part for their winning.

There it was again words, words, words, my mind screamed. Lucky, how can I be lucky? Doesn't he know Jennie's dead?

I yelled, "Get out, Gene, get out! Get out of this house!"

Janet came running in and escorted Gene out then came back saying, "This is getting scary, Dad. We are all in pain but it's not the world's fault and blaming them isn't going to make the pain go away. I think maybe we need to get you some professional help."

Eunice, who had just came in, said, "I think you might be right,

Janet. It looks like Caleb is going to need some help to get a grip on himself."

The commotion had brought Josh into the room and he said, "You know, Aunt Eunice, Janet and I can stay for a couple of more weeks, so let's give Dad a little more time before we do something drastic. I have read that counseling and medications can be of help in these situations, but sometimes they have the opposite effect. I would rather see Dad struggle for a while now, than suffer malaise all his life. "

Wanting to escape all this talk of medication and doctors I ran to the bedroom. I threw myself on the bed thinking, not our bedroom any more, just my bedroom, *as I burst into tears. I couldn't stop. I just lie there in a bed wet with my tears until the next day. I heard them checking on me every once and a while but no one disturbed my torment.*

I might have dozed off some because the next day as I was showering I recalled hearing Jennie's voice during the night saying, "The children, Caleb, the children. You have to help the children."

The children were at the breakfast table in the kitchen, so I joined them saying, "I'm sorry that I haven't been much of a father for you two to lean on, but now that I've had a good cry, I'll get better."

Inside I didn't feel better but with Jennie's words: The children, Caleb, the children, *deeply imbedded in my mind, I knew that I had to at least play the part.*

For the next few days I started each day working to polish my act. I must have been doing well because Josh suggested I should call Ace, he didn't think I would need to apologize just alert them I was doing better.

Gene came to the phone and said, "Great, Caleb and as soon as you feel up to it come back and join us. "

I doubted that there was anything that was going to happen but agreed I would try. Josh and Janet were both so visibly pleased with my actions I decided I would go back soon so they would feel it was all right for them to go back to their life.

About a week later I called Gene and ask him to talk to the crew and explain that last thing I needed was a lot of talk about what had happened. After he assured me that he understood and would talk to the

173

help, I told him I would come in for a short stay the next day.

True to his word the next day outside of a few sorry for your loss statements, I didn't have to deal with a lot of verbiage. I sat for a little while in a meeting where they were discussing a television spot advertisement for some fruit drink.

Surprisingly I found myself writing things like,

Drink a glass of juice and see how wonderful it can feel

To get your daily dose of fruit and never touch a peel

I was quickly swept with a wave of guilt for that moment of frivolity. I abruptly left the meeting and went to my little office. I felt some strange relief in the return of my darkness and despair as I set at my little desk there. There was a comfort not to have to put on a front while I was hidden.

I was surprised at the time when Gene rapped on the door saying. "We're closing up for the day Caleb, are you ready to go?"

When I arrived home Josh said, "Must have gone alright Dad, we didn't expect you to stay all day."

Janet came in and after giving me one of her deep inquiring looks said, "I know how hard it is, Dad, but I'm proud that you are attempting to move on. Josh and I will be leaving next week and we are both going to feel more comfortable now that you are returning to work."

I hadn't really given returning to work much thought, my thinking had been more on the lines of just getting the children feeling good about me and letting them get back to their lives. Still the solitude of my little office was a welcome respite from charade I was trying to live.

So every day I went into Ace, I knew I wasn't contributing much but it didn't seem to bother anyone there. I had only planned to go to Ace until after Josh and Janet left but the morning after they flew out, Josh to Oscin to pick up his car to drive back to New York and Janet to join her husband in California, I found myself heading back to my office.

At the office Gene, who must have been rummaging around in my office, said, "Caleb I found that bit you had written about the fruit punch. Could you give it another go to see if you can make it a little smoother?"

Alone in my office I spent well into the evening playing with that wording and some of my other doodles. It had been a rule that nobody was to bother me while I was working in my office, so when I came out everybody was gone, I left what I had on Gene's desk and went home.

This was the first night I was alone in the house since Jennie's death and I found myself sitting on our sofa by the stove. It was very painful and I thought it would be better to leave. Instead I decided to stay and have a glass of wine like Jennie and I used to do.

After that night there wasn't any mindful thought to how I used my time, but it became my routine to go to the office every morning and come home at night to my couch and the wine. Eunice kept inviting me to her house for meals but I had refused or made excuses so many times, her invites grew less and less.

The weeks turned into months and I still couldn't shake my despondency, carrying it like a badge of honor. Some nights after drinking enough wine I would find myself talking to Jennie almost like she was there. Sleep had been avoiding me but some nights after drinking wine I would wake up in the morning still on the couch. Believing that I had found my crutch in the wine, I decided I needed some help at work, so I hid a bottle of vodka in my office. For over a year there were no real problems. They even were finding value in my writings at Ace and I thought. Why not, isn't it true that some of the world's greatest writers were drunks?

One night coming home from work late, I was stopped by the police and taken to the station charged with a DWI. Eunice came and got me and read me the riot act all the way to the house, she threatened to call Josh if I didn't straighten out. I lost my license for a year and Gene had to pick me up to go to work. Even he was getting on my case about my drinking and wouldn't stop at package stores for me. It didn't mater, I found a store that would deliver and was able to sneak liquor into my office among my papers and lunch I always carried.

One day Lonny broke the rules and came into my office, sitting on my desk he said, "Caleb we have to talk, I am a recovering alcoholic and if you want me to, maybe I can help you."

I laughed saying, "Are you accusing me of being an alcoholic?

175

Cause if you are, you're way off base, I can stop drinking whenever I'm ready."

"That's just the point Caleb, maybe I can help you in getting ready," Lonny answered.

Losing control because of his audacity, I yelled, "You get out Lonny, you just get out. I have to listen to enough of your stupidity in the meeting, don't you ever dare come in my office again."

That night when Gene took me home he said, "Caleb, I think you need to take some time off and get a hold on yourself. Your contributions have been way below par lately and what you did to Lonny today is inexcusable."

As I got out of the car I yelled, "So that's it huh, Gene? After carrying Ace and its lousy programs all these years, I get heaved out like some used coffee grounds. You can take your lousy job and you know where you can shove it. I don't need you or Lonny, or any of the rest of your damned company."

Gene, looking crestfallen, slowly drove away while I staggered up to the house. After finding my way to the couch and having a few more drinks, I talked to Jennie about the cruelty of the people in my world and how ungrateful they all were.

The next thing I was really conscious of was someone shaking me and saying, "Dad, Dad wake up."

When I came to, it was Josh shaking me. I'm not sure how long I had been lying around there drinking, but from the looks of things it must have been a few days. Josh helped me into the shower as I was finishing the shower I started to have the shakes, having experienced them before I grabbed the pint I had under the bathroom sink and had a couple of hard belts. That got me under control by the time Josh hollered he had breakfast ready.

At the table Josh said, "Dad, Aunt Eunice called me and seeing as I was out this way, I changed my route so I could stop and see you. I can't stay Dad, I'm in the middle of a big project and I have to leave tomorrow. I'm going to call around and see if I can get you into a rehab center around here before I go."

"Rehab center, Rehab center, don't you mean one of those kill or

cure places that Uncle Louis used to talk about. Let me tell you something, Josh, there isn't any way that that's going to happen," I shouted.

I started eating the breakfast he had prepared as I heard Josh slam out the door. I was surprised at how hungry I was, must have been a while since I had eaten.

Josh was gone for quite a while and by the time he came back with Eunice I taken a couple of more big hits on the medicine in the bathroom and had called the package store for more. The delivery came when Josh and Eunice were telling me all the things that I was going to have to do. When Josh saw what was being delivered he rushed out telling the man he would have to take it back.

To me that was the last straw, so I yelled. "Who the hell do you think you are? This is my house and no damn son or sister of mine are going to come in and run it for me. If you don't like the way I do it just get out and stay out."

Josh started to come to me saying, "Now, Dad."

Eunice cut him off saying, "No, Josh, let it go. We'll do just as he says and get out of his life forever if that's what he wants."

I didn't respond, Josh with Eunice's arm around him and tears in his eyes got into her car and left. Josh must have cleaned up the room where the stove was because when I got back to the couch, the room was cleaned and straightened up just the way Jennie used to do it. This was too much, so I poured myself another drink and threw myself on the couch and cried.

The next time I came back around, it wasn't because someone was shaking me but that in my fog I sensed a presence. I'm not sure how long he had been there but when I shook the cobwebs from my mind Homer was setting there drinking a cup of coffee.

He smiled and said, "Would you like a cup, Caleb?"

I knew that I couldn't hold a cup without shaking, so I said, "I think I need something stronger than that Homer. What the hell are you doing here anyhow?"

He handed me a glass half full of whiskey and after I had downed it

177

he said, "I was just wandering around this part of the country and needed an inexpensive place to stay, so I thought I'd come and bunk with you for a while."

I didn't know whether this was the truth or not but there was some strange comfort that he was here, so I didn't challenge him. Homer seemed to just settle in and though he never said a word about my drinking and even would have a glass with me sometimes, he insisted I eat regular meals. He talked to me a lot.

He talked about Sterling, about working at the cow barn, about Arthur, Janet, Jennie and all of the crew we used to work with. He talked about his kissing club, about my fishing trips, about climbing on Mount Fay, about being in the tower when the state firewatcher was there.

Sometimes I found my self-joining in to correct something or adding to his story. With Homer there I no longer drank myself into oblivion every night though I kept a healthy buzz on. By the time Homer had been there a week I was looking forward to our everyday childhood reminisces.

Much to my surprise one night I said, "Do you think I could ever go back Homer?"

Homer laughed saying, "Well I can't make you young again Caleb, but if your heart is still in Sterling, if you're willing to work hard, maybe I could help you at least get back to Sterling."

Homer's visit and his stories had produced a flickering of light in my dark despair, so a few days later I asked. "What would I have to do Homer?"

Homer looked at me for a moment then said, "Do for what, Caleb?"

"Go home to the Sterling of my youth Homer, where I can maybe find a place to hide from this pain," I answered

"That's the work part Caleb. You are going to have to deal with the pain first or there will never be a place to hide. Not here, Sterling, or any place in the world. Homer answered sternly.

"Your talks have made me see dimly through the fog that there is life out there worth living. I'd like to try to get there, will you help me, Homer?" I asked.

"I can help you get started, Caleb," Homer answered, studying me carefully, "but you have to understand that nobody can do it for you. There's help but in the end you have to conquer all your demons yourself."

Homer must have been planning for this day because shortly after I told him I wanted to get started he was enrolling me in the detox unit of the local hospital. They kept you partially sedated while they ran tests to see how much of your body had been effected by the alcohol so it wasn't too bad there.

After I had been there for a few days Homer, who hadn't been in before, came in with a Dr. Bob, a psychiatrist.

Homer introduced him saying, "Caleb, the doctor is going to ask you questions that will determine what is the best treatment in your case."

The doctor asked questions for a long time, questions like how many children were there in your family, did your parents have any favorites, did you ever hate any of your brothers or sisters.

He went on and on like that and then he said, "What are you thinking, Caleb?"

I said, "I'm thinking: what do I have to say or do to get out of here and get a drink."

He never blinked, just kept asking questions. But seeing the shock on Homer's face, it dawned on me what I had said. After about another fifteen minutes of questions the doctor and Homer left.

Homer came back and said, "Tomorrow Dr. Bob is coming back to discuss your options. I hope you realize that this detox unit is probably only the beginning Caleb. Are you prepared to go the distance?"

After Homer was gone that day, my mind fluctuated between being puzzled by all those questions and fighting the desire to drink.

The next day Homer came in right after lunchtime. He said after evaluating yesterday's session, Dr. Bob has suggested that I enter a controlled rehab for at least a month. He said he saw a real desire in me to sober up but that I would not probably be able to control my desire to drink without further help.

"Eunice had already checked into one in Lotus and after talking to her and them, I think that is where you should go."

At first I couldn't speak. I kept thinking: A whole month of rehab, the kill or the cure, the whole degradation of it. *I thought as I remembered Uncle Louis's distain for places like that. Then I recalled what Dad had said about booze ruining most of Uncle Louis's life.*

Thinking, My God, I'm going to be just like him, *with my head in my hands I said, "Homer, I feel the want more then the hurt. If you promise me you won't lose me there, then I'll go."*

"I promise Caleb, I'll be there every day they let me visit and I want you to know I have never been more proud of you then I am at this moment," Homer answered.

The next day I was transferred to Lotus Rehab Center. There was more freedom there so I was allowed to go outside and walk the grounds as long as I made all the meetings I had been assigned to attend. I had a complete physical and there were some concerns about the condition of my liver, but the doctor said it was a wait and watch it situation.

I had to go for counseling three times a week privately with a doctor and every day the rest of the week in a group session. Every night they held AA meetings and we were required to attend at least four a week. My first impressions were: I am not like them at all, but little by little as I listened to their stories, I began to see parts of myself.

In my sessions with the psychologist we explored the darkness that I still carried from losing Jennie. The first session was a three-handkerchief job as I poured out my pain.

After a couple of sessions, the doctor said, "A case like yours could take much longer, but we only have a month so let's cut to the chase. I have listened to your reasons for becoming an alcoholic, but as you'll hear often in the program, they're not reasons, they are excuses. Excuses so you don't have to face the facts of your life as they are."

"You want to blame God and the rest of the world because that is easier for you. If you were God, would you change what happened? No, you wouldn't, because you would have already given us free will and our free will is what controls what happens here on earth, not God. I want you to think on this until next time you come. Try bringing it up in the group sessions, bat it around for a few days then we will discuss it again."

I did mention it in our group and it was amazing watching others struggling with the truth of it. As the days wore on, little by little, the impact of my sessions with the doctor and the group meetings brought a startling clearing in the way I had been thinking.

Like he had promised, Homer had come every day except the first few days I was there and that was because the doctors advised him not to. By the end of the second week, Gene or Lonny from Ace were coming in every couple of days.

I was uncomfortable at first with Lonny but he just laughed when I tried to apologize for our last meeting, saying, "No sweat Caleb. After all, this was my home away from home for a month about ten years ago. My life now makes me happy that I came here. I know it saved me from a personal hell of my own making. We have kept in touch with your brother on how you've been doing and from what he's told us, you're starting to see there's a light at the end of the tunnel."

Gene was more businesslike.

He said, "Caleb, from what your brother tells us, you might be leaving this neck of the woods someday. I hope you will find it in your heart to give us a few weeks before you go. We hired a couple of writers and they quit after only a couple of days. We have one now that looks like he might stay but he needs a lot of polish before he reaches the heights we have come to expect since you've been there."

"I think I'll be able to try and help you with that, Gene. I have discussed leaving here in counseling and their advice is that I should stay in my same environment for at least six months after I get out of here," I answered

During my time with Homer, we always spoke about Sterling and all that had happened back there when we were young.

One day Homer said, "Caleb, I have looked all over your house and I couldn't find anything but a few notes on the novel you told me you were writing."

It was with a pang that a vague memory came to me of burning those writings in the stove in a drunken rage not too long after Jennie's death.

I said, "Oh my God, Homer. I think I burned everything, every last page."

Homer seemed to flinch a little, but he said, "Well, that will keep you out of mischief for a while, because you promised me I could read that book when you finished and I'm holding you to it. Still, Caleb this might even be a good thing now that you have a clear head; I bet you'll even do a better job when you get back to Sterling. After all there can't be a better way to write about a place than actually being in the area you're writing about. You are planning on writing your novel again, aren't you?"

"I'm not sure about that just yet, Homer," I answered, "in counseling they suggested that I don't make that my primary concern right now. Not that I shouldn't write but I should wait for six months of sobriety before I tackle anything that as frustrating as writing a novel can be. I feel in my heart that I will want rewrite and finish the novel I burned. Still, right now, I need to concentrate on what I have learned here until I'm sure I can control my addiction."

The night before I was discharged from the rehab center, they put on a special dinner for those of us leaving, allowing us to invite all our friends. Eunice came with her son Hank who was now a senior officer in the army, and was home visiting Harry. Homer, Gene, Lonny and several others from Ace came, too.

It was a very meaningful evening; especially since so many from Ace came, they all asked how soon I would be back to join them.

The next day I left the rehab with instructions to make sure I attended an AA meeting that night. The group from Lynbrook had held their meetings at the rehab the last week I was there and one of their members, Tom, had offered to be my temporary sponsor when I got out.

Homer and Eunice came to take me home and when we got to my house I was glad I wasn't alone because I could sense Jennie was everywhere. I now knew that I could no longer hide from this so I spoke openly to them about it.

Eunice said, "After mother died, even though I had been away from her for years, I would sometimes have a feeling that she was watching me and guiding my feelings. It was eerie at first but eventually I came to see it as a good thing. It only happens now when I'm under extreme stress and believe me, it's welcomed."

Since this seems to be let's be honest day, *Caleb, I have a confession,"* Homer said quietly. *"You aren't the only one in the family who has had to wrestle with the demon booze. I was pretty much lost in the bottle just before Dad died. About a month after his death, one night when I was drowning my sorrows, I must have fallen asleep. When I woke up I swear Dad was in the room with me pointing his finger and saying, 'Homer you're more of a man than that bottle. Do something about it.' Every time I picked up a bottle after that, it was like I could hear him again, so I joined AA and after six or eight months of meetings and a good sponsor, I became a completely sober alcoholic."*

Things were tough sometimes for the next couple of months, some nights I would wake myself screaming. I would be covered with sweat and vaguely remember trying to save Jennie from fires or accidents or falling off a cliff. Homer was usually there to talk me back and the few times he wasn't I called Tom, my sponsor. He was a rock no matter what time of the day or night I called. He would either come to me or advise me on what to do.

Things went well at work. Gerry, the writer they had hired was all right. He just needed to understand how to approach the crazy meetings with an open mind. I showed him some of the crazy doodles I came up with in those meetings and how we weeded them down to the wording that ended up in the ads.

Josh had been able to stop by a couple of times, it was good that we had time to talk now that I was sober. He was ecstatic that I might be moving back to Sterling, saying he often thought he would like to retire there himself. We talked about the property in Lynbrook and he thought it would be best if I sold it.

Janet was able to come and spend a week with me she also thought it was a good idea to sell the house if I moved. We talked about Jennie and what she would think about my going back to Sterling.

Janet knew her mother wouldn't have wanted to go back if she was still with us, but she said, "Dad, I have to tell you, when I left last time I felt like I had lost both of my parents. When I held you the day I left, I could sense your darkness and feared I was losing you too. I sent you letters but you never answered, Eunice kept us informed but from what

I hear now, she sugarcoated it, even though she did say she thought you were becoming an alcoholic. My husband said there was no way I could help you until you were ready to ask for help. Homer answered some of my letters after he came here and told me not to worry. You would be ready in time. He was right."

"These last few days have made me so happy. When you talk about Sterling and Mount Fay, I feel like I used to when I was a little girl sitting on you lap hearing those tales. Now I will be able to leave here with such a weight lifted from my mind."

I had been out of rehab over four months when Janet left and I started to make plans for my trip back to Sterling. I had several offers for the property though I hadn't even advertised it yet. In my mind there was a lingering guilt about selling something that had meant so much to Jennie.

At work, the architect who occasionally worked there had drawn up plans for me from pictures and descriptions I had given him of the house that had burned in Sterling.

The realtor in Sterling, who had bought the land for me where our house that burned once stood, told me I wouldn't be able to build something like that today because there were new laws regulating what and how you could build. We decided to have a garage with kind of an apartment built there instead, until I could be there to get something near what I wanted built.

My craving for drink was no longer a problem that occupied my mind but selling the house that Jennie so loved still haunted my thinking. Though I still occasionally dreamed of Jennie, it wasn't always an unpleasant dream.

One night in my dreams she was telling me: It's time Caleb, go back to your mountain. I can be there too if you ever need me.

The next day Eunice called. She knew a young couple that wanted to see the house. She showed the house while I was at work and they fell in love with it and came to see me that very evening. They were so young and they had a little girl named Jean about three years old. As she ran around the house it was like when Janet was that young. I felt that Jennie was by my shoulder whispering: They're the ones Caleb, they're the ones.

The said they needed some time to sell land they had bought before they could raise the money to buy, but begged me to hold the house for them. Though I had already bought tickets to leave in two weeks, I told them they had a deal.

Homer, who had been spending time at Eunice's helping with Harry, said he would take care of the sale and the property for me, although I would be needed for the closing. This couple and their little girl had given me freedom from guilt about selling.

During the next couple of weeks, I cleared up all of my loose ends and finally found myself on the plane headed back to Mountain Road in Sterling dreaming about Mount Fay.